AF552431

INTO THE OBLIVION

INTO THE OBLIVION

Dr. A.P. Maheshwari
Vineeta Chandak

Ocean Books Pvt. Ltd.
ISO 9001:2008 Publishers

Published by
Ocean Books (P) Ltd.
4/19 Asaf Ali Road,
New Delhi-110 002 (INDIA)
Phone: 011-23289777
e-mail: info@oceanbooks.in

ISBN 978-81-8430-286-8
Into The Oblivion
by Dr. A.P. Maheshwari and Vineeta Chandak

Edition
First, 2014

Price
Rs. 250.00 (Rs. Two Hundred Fifty only)

Printed at
Bhanu Printers, Delhi

Dedicated to our Mother

Late Kamla Devi

who is the 'anchor' of this tale and the intrinsic philosophy of life emanating from it.

FOREWORD

I consider my privilege to write foreword for 'Into The Oblivion'. At the outset it is an interesting detailed description of family bonding, public healthcare system and emotional issues originating on way to deal with illness over a period of time treatment is underway, palliative care towards end and above all faith in one's own beliefs.

Let me discuss all these issues one by one. A mother, of 4 children, three sons and a daughter, has been discovered to be suffering from a lump in one of her breast. Authors have done a commendable justice to write in an understandable English language every major or minor detail right from the diagnosis and multimodality management of the illness. While reading the script one gets the feel that it is happening in front of the eyes and whole scenario rolls around happenings. The description helps to create awareness about access to healthcare and its limitations as it stands today. Importantly, it brings about certain controversial aspects of healthcare delivery to the extent that physicians could guide by unethical practices while making decisions about newer medications.

Much more important, I consider this chronicle brings about intimate bonding between mother and children both sons and daughter. The present compilation of the 'Into The Oblivion' is a true testimony that a 'devout Son' and a beloved daughter have decided to pen down their memoirs as the mother went through the ordeals of diagnosis, surgery, chemotherapy and finally palliative care. When everyone in the family including the patient were feeling relieved with the impression that 'Mayan' (Mother) has been cured or at least her disease has been controlled, suddenly recurrence haunts the patient and the family together. Here began the last journey. It is commendable indeed how 'Mayan' (Mother Patient] came to the terms and withstood complexities of palliative care.

The book could serve as a guide for public at large telling about do's and dont's in the circumstances every family goes through such illness when someone near and dear one suffers. Even more important lesson one can learn how to respect and love one's own parents which is becoming a victim of modernisation of society and in the era of nuclear family system. I give full credit to 'Son Vineet' who deserves all due compliments for looking after the 'Mother Mayan' in such a way that she never expressed a feeling of 'Helplessness' or the son and daughter never gave her chance to feel of 'Burdensome/dependability' until she left for heavenly abode. We all know the absolute truth of life that is 'Death'. One, who is born, will die but we always feel sad whenever we lose someone near and dear one. To which I say why not, we miss them and cherish long association with good and bad times. If some one we loose while terminally ill, it is liberation (Mukti) of the self and those who are caring.

I would highly recommend reading of these memoirs written by a 'Devout Son' and a 'Beloved Daughter'.

(Dr. M.C. Misra)
MS, FRCS, Hon. FRCS (Glasg.)
FCLS, FAMS, FACS
Director
All India Institute of Medical Sciences
New Delhi

New Delhi
05-05-2014

A TRIBUTE

In every moment and amidst each thought,
more a friend, so strongly dependable;
eternally enthusing the courage to sail us through,
those moments of desperation so inescapable.

A smile all the time, in any situation be they howsoever deplorable,
like the lamp that survives a storm were her teachings indeed formidable.

Hungry till all her children had had their stomach full,
feeding, cajoling morsels to her child who played difficult still.

Spending endless sleep deprived nights just so she could have us up with the dawn of wisdom,
ushering us onto the path which was not part of the erstwhile freedom.

Shielding us from all those dangers, that life could spill,
we were chiselled and finely groomed to stand abreast with a strong will.

Pouring her love which soothened us as does the morning dew,
'how to say no' was a method she never, never knew.

Imbibing in us those values and lessons of integrity,
she prepared us to face any adversity.

Ushering us on beyond the rural bonds life drew,
she made us adept in the etiquettes that an urban life brew.

Brooking any old time restrictions,
she made our childhood brim with playful distractions.

Our family joys would know no limitations
when we returned with trophies and certifications,
each and every moment of life was anointed with
celebrations,
like a dancing peahen, nature's best creation.

Hidden deep within her remained her personal woes,
was ever ready to wipe off the tears of all, whether
a friend or a foe.

Told or observed untold,
she would endeavour to do, whatever she could within
her hold.

Howsoever colourless the canvass of life may unfold,
she would readily decorate it with colours ever so cheerful
and bold.

Whatever you did for us,
what you were and will remain for us,
yes all of that,
which we failed to express—
Oh Mother!

—Bimal Maheshwari
—Surat Maheshwari

INITIATION

To discover the complete truth is rare. Each individual imbibes from his own surrounding as per his cognitions, perceptions and inner realisations.

The present story is the writer's modest attempt to identify the truth that lies beyond the mere superficial. Hailing from a remote village, a young girl at an early age moves into a small urban town after her marriage. There her inner spirit blossoms thriving through the passing up and down swings of life. However, physically she fails, gradually losing to the vagaries of a terminal disease and finally goes down fighting a raging battle against 'Cancer'.

Simultaneously, while touching upon the intricacies of the treatment of 'Cancer', diverse psychological and behavioural dimensions of the patient, as well as her caretakers; the story also courses through the ultimate philosophy of life, which actually moulds the core of the very existence of its main character, Mayan. People close to her act as catalysts for her transformational processes. The multiplicity of positivities as well as negativities, that come to her as boon or bane, an acceptance or rejection, a state of turmoil or calm, finally transcend her to a state where she succeeds in blooming from within. Then she conquers her physical limitations through mental force and mental saturation via her infinite faith. She eventually takes that much coveted, giant, spiritual leap to pass gainfully through the 'Gateway of Oblivion'. We all strive, throughout our lives, to attain this penultimate state of maturity in order to win in the race of life. It is a different matter altogether that how and what we decide becomes our ultimate goal in life. We find the protagonist of this story struggling relentlessly and leaving no stone unturned to successfully achieve the culminating goal of her life.

'Mayan' is the generic name for 'Mother' in the state of Rajasthan in India, which also happens to be the native place of our main character. To attempt to define the term 'Mother' is to try to achieve the impossible. A mother is incomparable, her place in our life, irreplaceable. Mere words can never define her qualities. If we should look for an equivalent of a true benevolent spirit on this earth, then it is only the 'mother' who we find comes close, it is only in her that we can find those ethereal manifestations.

In case you are looking for sheer entertainment, this book may not be an appropriate choice for you. It is a thought provoking narration that carries this story to the higher echelons where it no longer remains just a mere tale. It would then depend upon the reader himself to ascertain his own level of interest. However, please give due recognition to my submission to this effect.

In this exposition, certain generic terms have been used which come from the local dialect of Rajasthan and Uttar Pradesh. Similarly, certain technical and medical terminologies have also been used. However, for the ease of understanding, their nearest meanings are to be found in the glossary.

In my attempt to depict reality through my perceptions, I have traversed across certain zones of imagery too. Hence, I tender my due apologies for any inconsistency, paucity of thought or a deficit of expression, which if any, I know for certain, are unintentional and certainly not otherwise.

The saga of 'Mayan' was originally published last year in January 2013 and released during Jaipur Literature Festival by Ira Pande. The English version is now being presented with powerful expressions and modulations, as appropriate, for which I would like to give the entire credit to my sister Vineeta Chandak who put in her heart and soul to bring alive the protagonist.

–Dr. Anand Prakash Maheshwari

Agra
6th July, 2014

1

Man really is nothing beyond a complex bundle of emotions. Different phases of his life make him enact different roles and reflect the varied shades of awareness. Our world in the true sense exists within us and us alone. All that we get to see beyond is meaningless and so futile. That which becomes the most coveted and the most beautiful 'home' for one, may remain just an unfulfilling abandoned abode in the eyes of another.

Some unknown fear had shaken her out of her troubled sleep. She sat up, covered in sweat, her clothes sticking to her, and sweat pouring down her sides. A succession of spine chilling shivers ran down the middle of her back accentuating her relentlessly growing fears in the middle of that dark, threatening and unforgiving night.

Her heart-wrenching sobs swept through the dominating silence in that menacing darkness of the night dispersing that eerie quiet with her woeful urgings for help, "O God Almighty! What have I done to deserve this?" Her uncontrollable cries reached out to her son, sleeping next to her. Waking up with a sudden jolt, a little clueless and still grappling to shake off that lethargy that sleep induces, he mumbled, "Maa, what is it?"

She responded flinging her arms around his neck and holding on to him tight, as if her very life depended on it. Her irrepressible sobs continued to shake her frail frame as she clung to her son, sinking her head deep against his firm shoulders as if desperate to draw from him some ounce of sustenance.

Then sensing the concern that was writ across her son's worried features; she could no longer restrain her wrought up emotions that finally burst in a fresh deluge of tears.

Her desperate cry for help probably could not traverse beyond the four walls of that room in the flat of a government colony. Swallowed up by the constant grinding echoes of the trucks plying on the busy streets across, her painful urgings failed to cross that long winding stretch, to move her near and dear ones who also happened to reside in that emotionally starved city of Delhi.

Overnight, everything had changed. Only ten days had gone by when she had cheerfully left for Haridwar. For the last 2-3 years, she had been making these regular trips to the Parmarth Ashram in Haridwar for complete body rejuvenating sessions. She had begun to look forward to these relaxed holidays where she enjoyed rediscovering herself in the midst of those invigorating spas, weight reduction measures and natural remedial sessions in order to provide some relief to her persistently niggling body aches and pains. The ashram was adequately equipped with a very devoted and responsible staff that took exceptionally good care of her. Her friendly and unpretentious disposition had also helped in making her very popular amongst them. They endearingly addressed her as 'Hamari Mataji' (one's own mother). She just had to set foot within those premises and the entire staff would appear from nowhere running to greet her with folded hands, "Pranam Mataji (regards mother!), it is so lovely to have you back."

However, somehow, this time she had felt a strange disinclination to go alone and so had goaded her daughter Anjali to accompany her. "Anjali, this is an experience that will do you a world of good. You will find yourself wanting to go back again and again every year, as every time you will come back feeling like new!" Anjali had then good-humouredly acceded to Mayan's persuasion and, so here, they were! The city of Haridwar holds a disarming charm of its own. Situated on the bank of the calming waters of the river Ganges against an imposing backdrop of the mighty 'Himalayas' and its breathtaking beauty in its natural grandeur, it casts a magical charm on all and sundry. Each individual who visits these holy shores returns substantially evolved and suitably chastened.

This centre of the holy faith makes no discrimination and nurtures both the devotees as well as the fraudulents alike.

On starting with her routine treatment sessions on the very first day, Mayan's lady masseur noticed a distinct lump in Mayan's breast. Concernedly she enquired, "Mataji, since when have you had this lump?"

"Probably, since the last couple of months."

"Did you tell somebody in the family?"

"No, should I have?"

Realising it was not in her place to express an opinion any further, the masseur fell silent, "No, not really."

"Oh, it's no big deal, I have been applying hot fomentation regularly during my bath. You will see it will be gone before you know it," came Mayan's playful assurance.

However, several conflicting thoughts were now coursing through the masseur's mind. "How do I tell this unsuspecting gentle 73-year old lady what could be the repercussions of a lump in her breast? O dear God! Please have mercy on this poor soul."

Continuing the exchange she further queried, "Who all are there in your family?"

And that started Mayan off on her pet subject, "You know what, my husband is a retired government official.

One of my sons too is a very senior police officer and my other two sons, they are engineers working with very reputed companies." And then she went on and on about the uniqueness of her family.

Probably the masseur would have wondered how a lady hailing from such an educated background could be so ignorant regarding the possible magnitude of her own problem.

Then it suddenly struck the masseur that Mayan was not alone but accompanied by her daughter. She immediately proceeded to inform the daughter about her concern and advised her to take this matter up immediately with the presiding doctor in 'Parmarth Ashram'.

Responding to the gravity of the situation and the need for an immediate course of action, Anjali without any further delay consulted the resident doctor and then proceeded to call up her brother in Delhi, "Vineet, we are returning to Delhi today."

Vineet reacted in consternation, "Why, what has happened?"

"Hey! Do not panic, this is just a precautionary measure. You see, the masseur has noticed a lump in Mayan's breast today during the morning massage session. Mayan says that it has been there for atleast the last 2-3 months. Then I also felt it. Just look at how careless Mom is, she did not even feel the need to tell us about it. She is still just making light of the whole issue saying, "Oh! I am pouring hot water on it religiously; you just watch it will subside in a few days. However, I seriously beg to differ. We should not now waste any more time. Immediately, line up a consultation with a specialist and seek an appointment with the Doctor for today itself. The lump could mean anything brother," pushed an anxious Anjali.

"Fine, where are you getting off once you reach Delhi? The car will be there to pick you up. In the meantime, I am lining up an appointment with the Doctor," said Vineet.

Vineet then proceeded to call up a doctor who was an old acquaintance. Delhi being a big metropolitan city one finds oneself generally at a loss of how to begin and where to find a doctor who would give sound advice. Therefore, a doctor friend seemed the best option to begin with. The doctor confirmed, "I sit in my clinic till the late hours. Please just get Mataji as soon as she reaches Delhi, I will see her."

Delhi becomes chaotic during the evening hours. It is as if the entire city descends upon the streets. Unending lines of streaming vehicles, each trying to overtake the other, lead to terrible traffic jams and congestions. The traffic lazily moving through the streets, with the deafening blaring sounds of aggravating horns, the stifling smoke emanating from the petrol guzzling tankers lumbering past, makes reaching one's destination truly an uphill task. Mayan had reached Delhi but the journey from the bus station to the doctor's clinic was full of hurdles and seemed herculean. An already exhausting journey had considerably sapped Mayan's energy, and then this tedious traffic was certainly not making things any easier for her. Along with that a growing anxiety to reach the clinic on time was adding to Anjali's irritation too. Vineet was monitoring their entire progress, ensuring that the driver took the side lanes, bypassing the main traffic congestions. Mayan too was now a little apprehensive, so she agreed to first head for the doctor's clinic. There was now also a need somewhere deep within her to get to the root of her problem.

As it is, they had been travelling for the major part of the day for this purpose. So, in any case it made more sense to get it over and done with first and then finally head home to turn in for the night.

By the time they finally reached the clinic it had become rather late. All the other patients had left and there had been persistent calls for the doctor from his wife to enquire how soon he would be leaving for home. Nevertheless, Vineet's urgent requests kept the doctor waiting.

Vineet hurried down the steps to receive Mayan as she got down from the car. Her eyes seemed to search deep in him for an assurance that everything would be all right.

Spontaneously responding to her need, Vineet hugged her tightly and whispered reassuringly, "Don't worry Ma, it is really nothing. Since a doubt has been raised we're just ensuring that it is cleared, that is all."

Mayan looked up, carefully surveying the clinic and its surrounding premises. A name plate strategically positioned was there, announcing that it was Dr. Rajesh Gupta's clinic. Through the half-ajar door, she caught sight of the unoccupied chairs provided for patients to wait outside his consultation room. Mayan walked up the small flight of steps with the support of her stick on one side and Vineet's shoulder on the other to reach the doctor's cabin.

The doctor immediately got up to welcome Mayan and offered her a chair saying, "Mataji, please take a seat." In the meanwhile, Anjali had also got off the car and quietly followed them into the room. Vineet introduced Anjali to the doctor saying, "She is my elder sister." Anjali folded her hands to wish the doctor, but her eyes were actually pleading, "Please doctor look after my mother and keep her safe."

Dr. Gupta was a renowned physician, well known for his professional integrity. A seasoned doctor, he had quickly assessed his patient's mental condition. Realising she was in real need of his reassurance he proceeded to gradually set her at ease, making small conversation, asking about her health, how her day had gone and some such trivialities.

Mayan now gradually began to unwind. She was actually enjoying narrating to the doctor her experiences and some hilarious anecdotes during her recent stay in Haridwar.

Then a peon in the doctor's clinic brought tea, and as he proceeded to pour the tea into the cups, Anjali, the protective daughter immediately cautioned him, "Please do not add any sugar in Mataji's cup."

"Why, doesn't Mataji take sugar?" the doctor queried.

"She is actually diabetic," Vineet extended the information in an undertone. Mayan was now back to being in her element, taking a sip of the tea she parried, "Don't bother to lend him your ear, doctor. It is a never ending list of ailments; if you should do so you shall never see its end."

The doctor was genuinely intrigued, "Well one could never tell. You look so absolutely fit and fine, Mataji."

Mayan had just finished her cup of tea and was now curiously observing her surroundings, the white washed walls, the clock on the wall announcing the lateness of the hour, 10.30 p.m. and next to it a calendar from some pharmaceutical company with a slogan that read "We only treat, it is God who cures." Mayan read the line very carefully and then directed a 'telling look' at the doctor. In the meanwhile, the doctor too had been carefully observing Mayan's reactions through his thick-rimmed spectacles. As their eyes made contact the Doctor suggested, "Mataji, shall I take your blood pressure?" The blood pressure turned out to be a little on the higher side, so the doctor thought it better to first familiarise himself with Mataji's entire medical history and then proceed with a thorough check up.

Vineet who had been a silent spectator all this while now intercepted, "I have all the details of her ailments till date. Around 15-16 years back she had suffered a mild heart attack. I do not have the medical papers at present with me but I remember it well, she has been a hypertensive patient ever since. Her thyroid has been playing up too and of course not to forget a slipped disc in her L-3 and L-5. She also suffers from a persistent rheumatic pain in her knees."

"Oh doctor I am such a mixed baggage of problems," Mayan good-humouredly intervened.

"Never mind Mataji, inspite of facing such issues, you still have such a brave and cheerful disposition," the doctor complimented her while continuing to type the details of her medical issues on his laptop.

Then there ensued a lull that was again broken by the doctor's enquiry about whether they had been maintaining a chart regarding her blood pressure and sugar readings.

"Well the blood pressure tends to go up to 160-170. The fasting sugar generally reads around 150 and the post prandial readings are generally around 250, though I am on medication to control them," Mayan elaborated while turning towards Anjali to reach out for her carry bag.

Mayan then went on to pull out her medicine kit from the bag announcing in her usual flippant manner, "Oh! I need only 14 such tablets every day to survive you know."

Vineet, for whom it was second nature to be meticulous and extremely well organised, had already been carefully maintaining her detailed medical file since the last several years. Realising the seriousness of her problem he had carefully preserved her X-ray reports as well. He then took out the records and slowly pushed it towards the doctor. He had chronologically filed all previous prescriptions. The doctor patiently browsed through its details while jotting down the relevant details for his own future reference. Then, turning his attention to Mayan he sombrely requested, "Mataji, now please could I see the lump?"

Feeling the lump he enquired, "How many days have gone by since you noticed it?"

"I think its about 3-4 months back when I first discovered it," was Mayan's reply.

"And you did not feel it necessary to show it to someone?"

"No doctor,"

"Why not, Mataji?"

"Well, because I sincerely believed that it would go away on its own. You see I have been regularly pouring hot water on it while taking my bath and have felt no pain or discomfort at all."

"Do you happen to have a cancer history?"

"No doctor,"

"Has anyone had cancer in your family?"

"Yes my mother had uterine cancer."

"Ah, yes! One more thing, now I recollect I had a small node like growth quite some time back under my chin," enlightening him she raised her chin to show the operation mark that was left after it had been removed.

"But the node had no malignancy and it was way back in the early eighties, around the time when 'he' was doing his MBA," Mayan elaborated pointing fondly towards her son, Vineet.

"Oh good! I am sure that even the present investigations will also show nothing to worry about. But just for the sake of our satisfaction I would like you to still get this check up done," the doctor made little of the issue in order to put Mayan at ease.

Dr. Gupta then asked Vineet to get an X-ray and a mammography done, adding, "Once the report comes we will be able to determine what needs to be done next. Please don't delay any further, make sure you get them done tomorrow itself."

Vineet had already asked Anjali to take Mayan to the car while he had stayed back to have a word with the doctor privately. The doctor confided in Vineet, "This could be serious, I feel you need to consult a specialist in the 'All India Institute.'"

Then after having thanked and taken leave from the doctor, Vineet joined Mayan and Anjali in the waiting car. Mayan immediately enquired, "What did the doctor have to say?"

"Oh nothing that is worth a mention, ma!"

"Are you sure you are not keeping something from me, Vineet?"

"No, no and just why would I?" reacted a worried Vineet.

However, the mother in her had accurately read the worry writ across her son's face. Mayan then forgot all her own aches and pains, "Look, I do not see any cause to worry either. You know I have had similar nodes removed earlier, so why the anxiety?"

It was already past twelve in the night as the three of them headed towards Vineet's flat. The streets in Delhi never sleep; vehicles were continuously plying with several of them emanating blaring music, as they zoomed past with several groups of youngsters swaying in the throes of ecstasy with not a care in the world. In the background, the sound of the barking of stray dogs could be heard now and again. However, the three occupants of the car were completely oblivious to all this as they were deeply lost in their own troubled thoughts.

After a while, Mayan broke the silence, cajoling her two worried children, "Why such long faces? I am going to be just fine. There is nothing wrong with me."

But then, silence again engulfed them as each struggled with their private conflicting thoughts, each trying to assess what really lay in store for them in the near future. They were struggling to adjust to this unexpected turn of events.

On reaching the house, they slowly got off the car while Vineet quickly stepped out and moved to assist Mayan climb up the small flight of steps. As he moved to hold her, he sensed the feeling of loss and a growing insecurity in her. Though she was still attempting to put up a brave smiling front, yet unwittingly his grip on her shoulders tightened as if making a desperate attempt to reassure her.

Extreme exhaustion and the lateness of the hour had anyway killed their appetite, so neither of the three felt like eating anything. But on Mayan's insistence the maid served them each a glass of hot milk.

Finally, Anjali broke down. Vineet immediately rose to her support, "We have to keep our faith in the Almighty, all will be well; I assure you Anjali."

Mayan too had her own share of concerns, concern about what her husband would be undergoing far away from her, then she herself was not properly clued in with what was going on with her. She knew he would be very worried, so typically, forgetting her own worries she demanded of her son, "You first need to call up your father and give him the details; he will be anxiously waiting to hear from us."

Anjali responded, "Not to worry, dad had already called on my mobile and I have updated him with the proceedings."

It was really getting to be a late hour now, so Anjali took Mayan to their room to ensure she was made comfortable and able to get some rest. Vineet also retired to his room and gradually drifted off to sleep as he lay in his bed planning the arrangements for the following day.

As per her daily schedule, Mayan was up in the early hours of the next day. She completed her morning prayers and then around 7 a.m. walked into Vineet's room to wake him up. Finding him fast asleep, she sat down beside him looking at him lovingly with a gaze that was soaked in motherly tenderness and concern. Realising that he had had a very difficult and hectic previous day, very gently, she started pressing his hands and legs. Her comforting touch gradually drew him out of his deep slumber. Sensing her presence next to him, he opened his eyes and sat up. He heard Mayan saying, "Is everything fine, what is bothering you?"

"I am absolutely fine, just go and rest, you really don't need to take any stress," replied Vineet with an assurance.

Ignoring his concern, she suggested lovingly, "Let's all share a cup of tea together." A session of a quick cup of tea followed and then everybody rushed to get ready since they had to reach the hospital and get Mayan's tests done. Mayan was not supposed to eat anything until then, hence Anjali quickly packed some breakfast so that Mayan could eat after the tests were done as she was bound to be hungry by then. Everybody was going through their routine in the usual manner but inwardly there were unexplained emotions and threatening apprehensions churning within them non-stop. Each was silently praying to God to make everything like it was before.

All three of them engrossed deep in their own thoughts were completely unaware of the world around them. They were oblivious to the jarring sound of the running engine of their car, the brilliance of the sun streaming down its rays filtering through the glass panes, the streets passing them by as they headed towards the hospital. The crowds were now growing, the milieu now reaching out to them and they were struggling to break free and breathe easy again.

Finally, they had reached the well-acclaimed All India Institute that they had heard so much about but never until then had they had any need to visit. Today they stood here at its threshold, inside which lay the mystery of Mayan's fate.

The place was milling with unknown faces. Faces of the rich and the poor looked alike, desperate in their efforts to ensure the well being and recovery of their loved ones. The multi-storey building was an intricate maze with myriad corridors that seemed to go on and on endlessly. Vineet rang up the concerned doctor to ask him for the directions to his cabin. Just then, Vineet's subordinate joined them. He had been sent earlier to familiarize himself with the procedures of the hospital. He guided them along, making way as they moved slowly to the lift that would take them to the third floor where Dr. Anupam's cabin was located. They had to wait for a while, as the doctor was already in consultation with a patient.

Mayan was curiously watching the other patients around them and then sharing her observations reassuringly with Vineet and Anjali, "Don't look so tense, I am fine. God is always there, looking after us." Probably, she was also attempting to draw reassurance for herself to brace herself for what was yet to come.

Meanwhile, the doctor's assistant called for Mayan. Opening the door, the three entered the doctor's cabin. Attired in his white coat, with his thick-rimmed spectacles perched precariously on his nose, the doctor was busy on his laptop, probably feeding in the necessary details of the previous patient. Next to him was his assistant glancing through some papers. A strange calm seemed to pervade over the atmosphere in the room, which was heightened further by the stark plainness of the white washed walls. All three stood at the entrance with bated breath, anxiously waiting for the doctor to lift his gaze and acknowledge their presence. The framed degrees and the honours that eulogized the competence and the extent of the doctor's experience and stature further added to their reverence.

"Mataji, why are you standing? Please come and take a seat," said Dr. Anupam raising his head.

Vineet then immediately moved forward to shake hands with the doctor introducing himself and his sister, Anjali. After the initial formalities were over, Vineet handed over the medical brief prepared by Dr. Gupta to the doctor who went through it all very carefully. Then lifting his head he directed, "Mataji, could you please come and lie down on this table." Drawing the curtain Dr. Anupam then examined Mayan. The exchange between the doctor and the patient was audible to Vineet and Anjali. Dr. Anupam was a renowned breast cancer surgeon. Probably through that peripheral examination itself, he had accurately assessed the situation. Though to Mayan he said, "There seems to be nothing really to worry about. But let us play it safe and get some tests done. You are so fortunate that you have come before things could take a turn for the worse and then I am also there for you, so you do not need to worry at all."

Mayan nodded, "Yes, you and I both need not worry on that count. The Supreme Being is the most capable doctor and he is tending to us all. It shall only be his wish that shall eventually prevail."

"I couldn't agree more, Mataji. All you need to do is the 'Mahamritunjiya Jaap' and everything will be fine. After all, we doctors only treat the ailment, it is eventually, He, the Supreme Lord who actually cures," Dr. Anupam added.

Then directing his attention towards Vineet, Dr. Anupam instructed him to get the tests that he had written done immediately.

"We will wait for the results before we decide on the future course of action," the doctor instructed. As an afterthought he stated, "We could also get the mammography and the FNAC done for now and later if there is a need we will do a biopsy. Actually, I will myself take the sample for the FNAC to the lab. Could you please take Mataji immediately to the minor operation theatre? I will also join you. In the meanwhile, I shall give instructions for the mammography test but for that, you will need to take her to the next building. I will inform them so that Mataji will not have to wait for long." One could already feel how considerate and genuine the doctor was. He then proceeded to take the FNAC sample to the lab personally saying, "I don't want to take the risk of the sample getting changed. These people can get very careless and then make wrong reports. So I always make it a point to ensure that all the details of the samples are written right in front of my eyes."

Suitably relieved now, they thanked the doctor and took leave proceeding to get Mayan's mammography done. They were informed that the results would be available only on the following day.

The three were outwardly maintaining a calm exterior but inside they were desperately trying to fight off a conflict that was threatening to destroy their world forever. What if the reports turned out to be positive and it turned out to be cancer? What then? No, no that cannot happen. The tussle between hope and despair continued to unsettle them through the remaining stretch of the night.

Mayan was now beginning to sense that all was not quite well. The house phone kept ringing incessantly with relations and friends making frantic enquires. Vineet landed up spending the better part of the day extending assurances of Mayan's well being. But how does one reassure oneself when the facts point otherwise? Fighting a battle against such contradictory thoughts Mayan gradually drifted off to sleep. Exhaustion had finally taken over and lulled her physically into a state of deep slumber but the semi-conscious mind persisted to function. Disturbing thoughts and the approaching possibilities of having to part ways with her loved ones in the near future continued to agonize her semiconscious state of mind.

In the wee hours of the following morning, when the heart wrenching wails of his mother abruptly woke Vineet up, he found himself at a complete loss to respond. Conflicting thoughts raced through his mind as his mother clung helplessly to him. Should he wake up Anjali who was sleeping in the adjoining room? But she had barely slept, as the two had been sitting huddled together till the wee hours of the night pondering over the possibilities, each as perturbed as the other at the recent turn of events. The last two days had been a harrowing experience for Anjali, draining her both emotionally and physically. Rather than being of any help in pacifying Mayan she too seemed to be on the verge of breaking down, further adding to the complication.

Realizing now that he needed to tackle the situation himself, he decided to bring the issue under control by adopting a strict stance. Raising his voice, he sternly admonished Mayan,

"Is this the trust you repose in your 'Deity'. Bear with the situation. Patience is the need of the hour. Nothing can happen until 'He' wishes it so. If that is what 'He' has destined for you then so be it, even if it is something as deadly as 'Cancer'."

"It is not something I do not realize, my son. But my heart does not want to accept it."

"I understand. Yet, you must humbly accept and devote your waking hours from now on only in remembering 'Him'."

She held on to her son, hugging him tight as if desperately seeking some consolation, some reassurance from his presence. The constant state of anxiety had begun to add its own share of stress to her already traumatized fragile state, resulting in severe stomach cramps and discomfitting gas formation. Realizing her present vulnerability, Vineet gently helped her stretch out on the bed and then proceeded to press her aching forehead and limbs tenderly. He had only recently taken a course in acupressure, which he now applied to the best of his capability. Acupressure tactics and the linen cloth that Mayan had tied around her forehead seemed to be helping now as he gradually felt her body relaxing, announcing that sleep had slowly taken over her tired frame.

Any mishap or unforeseen happening generally takes us back several years in the past where all those pleasant, unpleasant memories, that are otherwise stowed away deep in the recesses of our mind, begin to resurface like a movie rewinding and then replaying itself out before our eyes. Vineet remained seated next to Mayan carefully observing her facial expressions as his thoughts now flitted back and forth.

Mayan hailed from an affluent Mahajan family residing in a remote small village of Rajasthan. An only child, her upbringing had been extremely indulgent in a warm protected environment. She remained completely ignorant and unexposed to the harsh and the stark realities of life. Yet she was truly a brave heart. Once, when some dacoits had attacked their village, she, still at a tender age, had along with her mother jumped off the first floor of her residence. In addition, showing exceptional temerity had resisted being taken captive by the dacoits. Unfazed by their threats, she had smartly outwitted them in a blazing match of words. The dacoits had finally taken to their heels and she had in the true sense of the word become the 'heroine' of the village.

This fourteen-year old teenager had been married off at that tender age when a child generally leads a totally carefree and happy-go-lucky existence.

Being wheatish complexioned in a society that was still obsessed with the fair skin, she had had to bear many snide and cutting remarks. Yet with her gentle, winsome demeanour accompanied with an openly honest and genuine concern for others, she had eventually won over the hearts and sympathy of all around her.

Vineet, who had spent most of his formative years in his mother's village living with his maternal grandparents, had many pleasant memories attached to his 'Nani's home'. In those times when families were large, it was a standard practice to send a few children to be reared in their grandparents' home and Vineet too had been no exception.

Since the very beginning, Mayan had always shared her childhood memories with her four children. Some were happy, some not so happy, some sour and some very sweet. Married to a government officer with a limited salary and four children, Mayan had had a lot of responsibility thrust upon her young shoulders. Her day would start off in the wee hours of the morning, with the filling of water in huge drums in order to meet the day's requirement, since the municipal water supply was typically unpredictable and quite temperamental. In these circumstances, she often had to walk a good distance to reach the village well, make many trips back and forth carrying several pots of water on her head. Following this was an unending list of other household chores like cooking, cleaning utensils, mopping the floor, washing clothes, dusting, the list was simply endless. So very often you could see her venting her growing frustration by vehemently clobbering away at that never ending pile of dirty clothes. And then, as if this was not enough to fill her daily scheme of chores, she also made a daily visit to the local market to purchase the daily provisions. She often took her young kids along, as she could not risk leaving them in the house all by themselves.

Mayan, who was the embodiment of the perfect selfless mother, would serve her entire family generous helpings of the vegetables she had cooked and if there was nothing left for her, which was often the case, she would scrape off the base of the vessel that had held the vegetable, add some water, salt, red chillies and lemon juice to it and fill her growling hungry stomach with two dry chapattis dipped in that 'so delicious and nutritiously enriched' gravy. Their hand to mouth existence had conditioned her to avoid any possible wastage. So even if the food had begun to show signs of turning stale, she would carefully trim the visibly affected portions and use the rest to fill up her revolting tummy. Little thought was then spared to consider that these leftovers were gradually brewing within her a formidable combination that would later manifest itself in her as a deadly 'cancer'.

Life carried on as a heady cocktail mix of the highs and the lows. Hardships and difficulties had become a welcome spice in her brave struggle to keep her family safely cocooned and to ensure that she provided a content and nurturing environment around them. Relatives, as is typical, continued to be an acrid mix of the sweet and sour, as the situations would best suit them. Nevertheless, in coping with all these multi-faceted relationships when, it was that diabetes and hypertension took over her neglected frame, nobody really kept any track. Along the way she also suffered a mild heart attack, her neck and the backbone had also weakened as she had become a prey to severe spondylosis. Arthritis then gradually spread its tentacles and gripped her knees, infact even thyroid imbalance did not spare her. Yet the sunny side of her temperament remained surprisingly intact. Probably, her complete devotion and belief in the 'Almighty' was responsible for her positive spirit. Her daily routine would include spending her morning hours praying and at night before turning in, she would unfailingly do penance for any possible failings committed during the course of the day. Another very vital part of her daily chores was to ensure that before she called it a day, she would go around the house ensuring that her husband and kids were comfortable and safe. It has always remained an inexplicable mystery as to how she still managed to be up and about, briskly attending to all her morning chores at the very break of dawn with a refreshed spirit and vigour even though her body had barely rested for about four to five hours. It was still fresh in Vineet's memory how if they fell short of fuel she would quickly make fresh charcoal balls and cook their meals on them. If it happened to come up in a conversation with the younger generation of the family, they would ridicule it making it appear as a ludicrous suggestion and laugh it off as mere nonsensical humour. Nevertheless, that still does not change the fact that her life had been a far cry from a bed of roses. A lot of her unrealized desires had remained unfulfilled yet she had never complained. It was not unusual for her to somehow meet the essential expenses of the household by taking a meagre loan from the neighbours and make both ends meet. To make it worse were all those barbed comments that came her way, targeting the loans that she had been compelled to take in order to keep their kitchen fire burning.

However, once her children stood on their own feet and started to earn, the situation began to ease. Then, occasionally she would gently take the liberty of expressing her aspirations, her long suppressed desires before her children, "Do you know that golden wrist watch that we saw in the market today, I had demanded it of your father way back, infact almost twelve years back. Your dad had also gone to buy it but it was far beyond our pocket so he had had to return without purchasing it." Even before she had finished narrating the incident Vineet, who happened to be then posted in Gorakhpur, had bought it from the market and promptly placed it around her bare wrist. The intense delight, the emotions that had then flitted across her face, the light that had lit her eyes cannot be expressed by mere words. It had become an inexplicable moment of thrill and contentment for Vineet that had now been carefully stashed away in his memory forever. Since then he had become particularly sensitive to her needs. Her children now consciously continued to put in that special effort to quench her pent up desires.

Mayan was particularly fond of travelling. No part of the country had remained unexplored by her, right from Kashmir to Kanyakumari. However, as was so typical of the housewives of those times, her cooking cans and provisions had to travel along with her on these journeys.

Therefore, along with her travelled a moving kitchen to all the places that she would visit. Whether expensive or otherwise her style of travel underwent no change. Another side of her life that remained forever unchanged was that she without fail would make it a point to travel at least five to six times in an year along with her entire family to Soamibagh, a religious place in Agra to participate in the 'Satsang', a holy custom, to serve her 'Isht', her 'God'. Her devotion to her deity always remained unshaken and resolute. This was one facet of her life, where there was no compromise despite the financial constraints. It was this very same Mayan, an epitome of dignity and restraint, a woman whose happiness was synonymous with that of her husband and kids, who could now find no solace in the 'same' and completely breaking down, had wept inconsolably till sleep had eventually taken over her exhausted frame.

Vineet was now seriously perturbed and no longer at peace. Several questions had remained unanswered today. The lump that the doctor had felt and sent for testing seemed to be finding its roots deep in his mind as well. The lump seemed to be at the threshold of threatening to shatter the fun-loving lifestyle that Mayan had always maintained despite the hardships. It was a threat that would gradually sap out all that happiness from her life.

Bitterness was now creeping in. The most unpleasant memories and moments seemed to be successfully piercing and threatening their so far simple and happy existence. Putting aside those aspects of life with their unanswered questions, Vineet consciously moved on to an indulgent mode and gently shook Mayan awake. He gave a fond peck on her forehead and began to cajole her, "You need to come out of your beauty sleep, Ma, its time to get moving". The clock across the wall was announcing 9 a.m. When exactly, the mother and son duo had switched roles, was difficult to pin point. Now Vineet was the indulgent mother pandering and tending gently to Mayan, the child. Man really is nothing but a complex bundle of emotions. Different phases of one's life make one enact different roles and reflect varied shades of awareness. Our world in the true sense exists within us and us alone. All that we get to see beyond is meaningless and futile. That which becomes the most coveted and the most beautiful 'home' for one, may remain an unfulfilling abandoned abode in the eyes of another.

□

2

It is not always feasible to define when more than the administering of medication, it is the care, the compassion, the patience and the identification of the psyche of a patient who is in the grip of a life threatening disease that provides true support to the patient.

The Ayurvigyan Institute was as usual teeming with millions. Once you enter its premises, the realization begins to dawn that the layman in India with his limited resources has very restricted number of venues open for any 'Specialist Health Care'. The poorest of the poor could be seen lined up in unending queues from the early hours of morning in the hope that their turn would eventually come to get treated. Private hospitals offer no such solace to this class, so much so that even the middle-income group blinks at the possibility of having to take treatment in these so called 'money sappers'. In case one has been admitted in these over-hyped hospitals one should be mentally prepared that the bills will run into several lakhs. For those in the lower income group, when faced with such situations, this institute offers a ray of hope of being fairly treated and of recovery, even if it means some inconvenience and juggling amidst the rows of ailing humanity to reach the doctors.

Remembering the Almighty, Mayan and her near ones entered the hospital. The building is a jigsaw of unending, winding corridors. With Mayan's chronic back and knee issues there was no other recourse but to arrange for a wheel chair. However, acquiring a wheel chair in the institute meant once again waiting for your turn to come to avail the facility. Foreseeing the problem Vineet had already outsourced a wheel chair. Vineet's elder brother Suneet too had now arrived. After hearing about Mayan's ailment, he was naturally perturbed.

Despite having reached the hospital punctually, reaching the doctor's cabin took another good twenty minutes. The doctor seemed to be waiting for them. On their entry into his cabin, he promptly left his seat moving forward to bend down to touch Mayan's feet. Then he proceeded to help Mayan to leave the wheel chair and sit comfortably on the patient's seat. Vineet was bemused by the doctor's extraordinary and unusual reaction. Was it just a result of his upbringing or had the charisma in Mayan's personality drawn him to her? He failed to realize that a seasoned and compassionate Cancer specialist had realized the soothening strokes that were necessary on his part and on the part of the patient's close associates to help cope with the trauma that the patient was undergoing.

"Pranam Mataji, there is really nothing to worry about. Your reports have come. They show only some small inconsequential nodes that will be removed easily. All that we need now is a small sample to be taken for a biopsy preceded by a simple P.E.T. that is, Positive Emission Tomography. Via this test we will inject a radioactive material into your body that will provide a complete picture by highlighting the cancer cells that will help us distinguish the exact areas and to what extent the cancer cells have already spread", Dr. Anupam explained patiently.

"And sir, regarding the biopsy?" Vineet enquired.

"Yes, that is very essential as mere mammography or FNAC does not give us a complete picture. If FNAC should be positive then further tests become mandatory. Even if this test report is negative, that does not suggest that cancer is not present as the presence of the nodes or the changes taking place in those nodes may not be successfully intercepted by these physical examinations. Here mammography imaging further helps. Then biopsy in the case of the breast cancer gives confirmatory results. That will help me to ascertain the extent of the removal process that will be involved and clearly define how widespread is the state of the cancer. There is however no need for you to panic. Leave it now to me to deal with the problem."

"We are grateful, sir. Our purpose was not to question your efficiency, it was just our anxiety that compelled me to enquire. Please do not take it otherwise."

"Yes, I understand. PET is an expensive procedure, but I believe that you are entitled to a complete reimbursement," now getting down to practical business, the doctor enquired.

"Yes sir that is an issue we do not need to take into consideration."

Though they had been careful to conduct this entire conversation in English, yet Mayan had possibly assessed the crux of the flow of the entire conversation between them. The doctor expressed his reservations about any further talk in Mayan's presence.

Immediately after the biopsy was done, Dr. Anupam, as he had done in the earlier test too, personally proceeded to hand over the sample for testing and ensured that in his presence the details of the case were carefully put on record. PET was also done. However, its report would be available only on the following day.

Next day the PET test report was made available. There was some satisfaction drawn from the report that cancer had not yet spread to the other areas of the body. However, the unfortunate news was that instead of the single node now, there were multiple nodes in that area. It was necessary to compare the result with the biopsy report, which still would take a couple of days to come. Now there was little option but to wait. However, with the present available reports Dr. Anupam had already concluded that surgery was necessary to remove all the nodes, as mere medication could no longer control the cancer.

Now Vineet had resolved that he would avoid letting others learn about the details of Mayan's case. However, things generally do not turn out the way one resolves. The word eventually spread through some indirect quarter. Tongues started wagging. People left no stone unturned to make it as spicy and juicy a gossip as it comes. Despite his best efforts, the word had spread like wildfire that Mayan had cancer. And then started the never-ending line of phone calls. Vineet's repeated requests to refrain from showing sympathy so as to avoid any unnecessary jolt to Mayan's psyche and add to her emotional stress fell on deaf ears. The next day itself a gentleman arrived unannounced at the doorstep and went straight into Mayan's room. He immediately involved her in an animated conversation where he began to grandly announce how well informed he was on the subject of cancer, "You will now have no option, but to undergo chemotherapy. It is a very painful procedure; you will even lose your hair..." Upset with the negative trend of the conversation, Vineet had had to have the gentleman physically removed from the premises. Privy to the suffering that such interludes were causing to Mayan, Vineet's stance now took a stiff turn.

On returning to her room, a pained Vineet saw that the interaction with the gentleman had quite visibly affected Mayan. The colour had completely drained from her face. She looked ashen. He could sense how she was getting hurt inside. Probably the visitor's words had permanently scarred her psychology doing irreparable damage. It was not that she had been ignorant about most of what he had said to her. Nevertheless, a fresh attack reopens the scar and the hurt then pierces deeper, often leaving behind a permanent wound. How does one make these so called well-meaning 'enemies' realize that a patient struck with such a lethal disease needs to be handled with the utmost care just like a new born being held fondly in ones loving, encircling arms.

Two days later the biopsy report came. The lumps screened through mammography now had their pathological reports too. It was an invasive mode of cancer, that is, it had the volatile tendency of spreading. In fact it had already progressed from grade-I to grade-II. It was also 'Her-2-neu positive'. The estrogen and progesterone factors were positive and negative respectively. The issue was far beyond a layman's comprehension. Vineet and Suneet sought an appointment with Dr. Anupam. Dr. Anupam strongly believed in the philosophy of honestly sharing the details of the real state of the patient with the immediate family so that they would not harbour any false illusions and infact brace themselves for the inevitable. Perhaps that is what sets a capable doctor apart from the crowd. Dr. Anupam painstakingly explained the details of the report, "Look, it is obvious from the report that this cancer is not localized. It has the tendency to spread. It is also referred to as 'Intrusive or Infiltrating Cancer'. It can spread to the other organs of the body through the 'lymph system'. To put it simply, it can course through, carried by the blood stream to the other organs. Fortunately, so far, it has not spread as is evident in the PET report and it is 'Her-2-neu positive'. The cancer is of an aggressive temperament but as its receptor is positive, the hormonal therapy will be effective. However, we need to begin with first removing the already present cancerous nodes through surgery. We will perform the surgery after three days. Meanwhile, have her admitted in the hospital tomorrow itself. I am writing the formal advice."

"Yes, Doctor," both the brothers looked visibly shaken for a few seconds but then collecting themselves concentrated on the detailed instructions of the doctor.

"I will take you now to our 'radiotherapy unit' and introduce you to the doctors that are incharge there.

We will need their services immediately after the surgery. Let Mataji come along as well," instructed Dr. Anupam.

They then proceeded to the 'Rotary Cancer Hospital' that was just two blocks away. Maintaining a brave front Mayan sportingly went along. As they crossed the common ward, the spectacle that slowly began to unveil before their eyes was to say the least quite unnerving. There was an unending line of radiotherapy patients lying in the corridors. The scene before Mayan's eyes was spine chilling. To put it mildly, there were burnt, charred, disfigured, discoloured patients being attended to by expressionless caretakers, resignedly accepting their loved ones' pathetic plight. Each had its own story to tell, some so heartrending that one felt forced to question God's justice.

"Why this, why? Just what terrible deeds had they committed that God had felt that this was their deserved destiny!" Mayan could no longer hold back her tumultuous emotions. Bringing the wheel chair to a stop, she began to question the patients. What had reduced them to this pitiable plight? Probably, along with her curiosity was the gnawing fear that was gradually taking hold of her, 'Would she eventually meet a similar fate too.' God and His ways are sometimes inexplicable.

An old hand in his profession, Dr. Anupam was well aware of what trauma Mayan would be undergoing at that moment. The whole purpose of this exercise had been to gradually introduce and mentally prepare her to what she might eventually face. Very gently prompting her, Dr.

Anupam led her on, "Mataji, you must be tired by now, so let us go to the consultation room and have a cup of tea".

Entering the consultation room Dr. Anupam gently prodded her on, "Look at it like this Mataji, you have indulged in none of these vices, you neither drink, nor smoke nor eat tobacco, yet you have got cancer. We have no other choice but to accept it as your destiny and God's resolve. You are not in any way responsible for it. 'He' who has brought this suffering upon you will also cure you of it. Do not give up your hope or question 'His' decision. 'He' is there to look after us all. And 'He' will take care of you too."

Mayan reacted in her usual cheerful demeanour, "No no, I'm not worried. After all as you have said 'He' is there above to take care of me and of course here, we have you."

Vineet, Suneet and Anjali who had been silent spectators all along now moved gently near their mother. They held onto her, comfortingly pressing her shoulder and extending silent support. Mother's love, as so rightly said, is incomparable and knows no bounds. Without their uttering a word to express their concern, she sensed the fear and worry that was written across their solemn expressions, and that made her forget her own fears. So putting up a gallant front, she declared, "As long as you are there to take care of me, I know that nothing can go wrong. Even death will be eventually forced to change its course and look for alternate victims. After all your mother is not to be taken lightly, she is made of stern stuff and you know that well, don't you?"

Even today, that particular day remains permanently etched in Vineet's memory and why ever should it not!

As the doctor enumerated the so-called reasons that generally lead to this state, none of which she had ever even remotely had anything to do with, the Doctor's words had now begun to hammer away and were slowly gnawing Vineet's insides. Was his mother paying for his vices? Was this God's way of making him do penance? Even to date, it remains unexplained just what had happened but then suddenly all base urges deserted Vineet. Nothing of those uncontrollable base desires now had a hold on him; it was surely nothing short of a miracle that had taken place that day. How many times in the past Vineet had resolved never to touch these sinful elements? He had even succeeded in giving them up for a couple of months but very soon he would be back to being a slave to them. His desperate efforts to give up would temporarily work but never for long. However, at this moment, finally 'Nature' itself seemed to have intervened and in a flash it had changed him forever. The urges had died an immediate death and now lay buried forever.

It is not unusual to have certain memories permanently sketched on our minds depending on the difference and the importance that they hold in our lives. Vineet, after finishing school got admission in a very reputed institution of Delhi University. Even then, the several so-called well-wishers had warned Mayan, "Seriously, it is just not wise to send your child away. There is a great likelihood of his falling into bad company. There are so many such horrific tales doing the rounds that may spoil his future forever." But Mayan's sharp retort had reflected her complete trust and pride in her children, "He is my child, how can he ever go off track. There is no way that he will let me or my milk down."

Youth is an impressionable age where it is not unusual to give into the available temptations, the luring attractions that are freely available. You may then gradually develop an addiction that later becomes difficult to let go.

Realizing one such failing in her son, Mayan had gently reprimanded Vineet, "Do you realize that this momentary satisfaction that you are drawing in the present may eventually leave you saddled with a permanent handicap. Give it the due consideration it deserves, my son."

As is typical of the youth, Vineet too justified his indulgence explaining it away with the lame excuse, "How do you say I am drawing satisfaction through this indulgence? On the contrary, this is what helps me to keep awake and stay focused for long hours on my studies."

However, that did not find favour with Mayan. She reacted, "Who do you think you are fooling? Don't you try to justify it. What is wrong will never be right. You are my son and I cannot let my son have such flaws and base tendencies. So what, if you should not succeed you will still remain my flesh and blood, my son. Nothing can ever change that."

Faith begets faith is what they say. Mayan was a living example of this dictum. For quite sometime, Vineet stayed preoccupied with his recent past. Several incidents continued to churn and flash past him, taking him back to his bygone days. Suddenly, Mayan's sharp reproach brought him back into the present.

After sometime they all headed back home. Pitaji was the first to be informed about the latest developments. Then it was about making the necessary preparations for the imminent surgery.

Anjali had accompanied Mayan for a few days to stay in the Haridwar Ashram. Who could have thought that things would be taking such a drastic turn? She suggested, "I think I'll stay back till Mayan's surgery is over. Then I will have to go home to deal with the issues there for a while. After that I'll be back again to keep her company."

Vineet agreed, "I think that is just fine. In the meantime, I'll go and get the ward booked while you make a list of the hospital requirements and pack them accordingly."

Suneet enquired, "Do I need to come along?"

"No, I'll manage. You plan out how we will take turns at the hospital. We will need to take turns in staying with

Mayan at the hospital. Ask sis-in-law too. Prepare a roster in the meanwhile," Vineet suggested.

Suneet agreed, "Don't worry, I'll do the needful. If you don't require my services for the next 2-3 hours, I'll go complete a few of my personal chores."

Then taking Vineet aside Suneet handed over some money, "Here is some cash, you will need it for the hospital bookings."

"I don't really need any for the present. If I should in the future, I will let you know." Vineet humbly submitted.

They were all worried and so anxious. Pitaji too had joined them in the meanwhile.

When Mayan had entered after marriage into her in-laws' home, two of her husband's nieces had welcomed her. So, automatically they had struck a special bonding. Mayan was then still a teenager, only fourteen years old. One of these nieces had settled down in Delhi permanently. Mayan always addressed her affectionately as 'Bayaji'. They had immediately bonded and over the years, their friendship had deepened. They always discussed and exchanged their happy as well as unfortunate moments, thereby drawing comfort from each other's company. Therefore, Vineet thought it only proper to communicate the facts of the situation to her. Bayaji immediately responded and henceforth made it a point to stay by Mayan's side as much as was possible.

Though Ayurvigyan Institute has been an established and well-acclaimed hospital, it is always sensible to crosscheck the line of treatment to be undertaken. If for no other reason, but for one's own simple satisfaction and reassurance that the course being pursued is the right one, or just to reassure, if there is any other alternate therapy available of which one may still be ignorant of.

Therefore, Vineet also consulted his cousin, Madhup. They had always been very close. The wife of a close friend of his cousin happened to be a cancer specialist working with a reputed hospital in Gurgaon. Madhup fixed up an appointment with her. Vineet and Madhup went along, carrying Mayan's reports. The doctor advised them to bring Mayan along the following day at the hospital. It was a super speciality hospital, in fact more of a five star set up with luxurious facilities. Hygiene standards, cleanliness were a pleasant sight but then nothing comes without a price. Anyways, it was more important to confirm the quality of treatment and the post operative care. After a detailed analysis, the consensus drawn was that the treatment prescribed at the Ayurvigyan Institute was the best track to pursue. However, this visit had made a difference. The cancer specialist in Gurgaon had given some information that was of great significance, "Look, I am sure you are not unaware of the fact that a clear guaranteed line of treatment to cure cancer has not yet been evolved in any part of the world. It is still a trial and error method based on the latest research and conclusions that have been drawn. If the given treatment produces results then we have succeeded in hitting the nail on the head for that particular patient. In fact, the research that has been conducted so far is applicable mostly to people in the age group of 25 to 50 years. There is not much data available for people not falling in this bracket. In fact, people beyond the 50 years age bracket who are handicapped with their organs' efficiency having already deteriorated continue to remain a question mark; so how such a body would react to the treatment still remains an unsolved riddle and their response is entirely on trial and error basis."

Gradually the gravity of the situation was beginning to sink in. Though so far, the one action that had become clearly defined was that the affected breast part had to be surgically removed immediately.

The date for the surgery was fixed. The doctor had clarified that post surgery the heart and the bones would have some side effects. Therefore, it was necessary that certain tests related to these organs should be carried out before the operation itself. These tests would later help in ascertaining the extent to which the body was capable of accepting the changes. Some blood tests were also done and some medication administered 48 hours prior to the surgery.

Vineet was considerably perturbed by these latest developments. He was wondering that earlier when they had separately consulted the doctor, he had advised them to only book the room for the surgery. If only he had then indicated about the 'bone density test' and the 'heart ejection ratio', they could have simultaneously carried out these as well. But to question the doctor's decision is unethical and above all one has to maintain an amicable coordination between the cancer surgeon and the cancer specialist as both play an equally critical role in determining the success of the surgery. One really has no option left but to willingly follow directions, in order to ensure the cooperation of the doctor and the well-being of the patient.

All the tests were now completed. The reports then followed and thankfully all the parameters turned out to be acceptable, so there was now no complication that could be foreseen in the performing of the operation. All preparations were on the go and clear directions were given for the following day's activities. Mayan was to have her meal by 7 p.m. and nothing following that. Whatever further requirements and preparations were needed to be completed, the necessary directions were handed out to the nurse on duty accordingly.

In the evening, the private ward was made available. Though the government hospitals provide the necessary facilities but, as one is well aware, hygiene still remains an undefined area that always needs personal attention and effort to ensure the desired quality of sanitation. Vineet personally ensured that the washroom and the private ward was properly resanitized and disinfected for his own personal peace of mind. The room, otherwise, was just fine, the walls looked like they had been recently painted in a neutral shade with the patient's bed placed against the wall, while a settee and a table combination had been provided for the attendant's convenience. The hospital had specific instructions that did not allow more than one attendant to stay on even in the private wards. Mayan, accompanied by her elder son Suneet, had moved in the previous night. Vineet and Anjali stayed on till late in the night looking into the last minute preparations. Anjali felt that she needed to stay back with Mayan. Then the final consensus was that it made more sense for her to come early in the morning as she may be required to stay on after the surgery was over.

The night carried with it multifaceted apprehensions. The uncertainty of the situation built insecurities in their minds but exactly when the fears were overtaken by slumber's call, it is difficult to define. As morning approached, the clock too now seemed to gain momentum.

□

3

'Faith' is what finally leads us beyond mere logic and reasoning. As if to draw sustained comfort, Mayan clung on to Vineet's hand as the wheel chair carrying her started to move on. Both Anjali and Suneet stood rooted to their spot in a last minute attempt to control their sudden surge of emotions.

Mayan had arisen very early that morning, taken her bath and was ready and waiting in the private ward allotted to her in the hospital. A firm follower in her faith she had offered her morning prayers and then proceeded to hold a normal conversation with her children in an effort to set their minds at rest. Her first and foremost concern was, as usual, her children and not the surgery she now had to undergo. Extending her final reassurance to her dear ones, Mayan bravely moved on towards the operation theatre.

"I am telling you this is the best thing that could have happened to me. Now I will get rid of this headache once and for all," Mayan said directing a reassuring glance towards Vineet who had continuously held onto her hand as though desperate to comfort her.

But as the stretcher moved into the 'No entry zone' Mayan turned back to direct at her children a parting expression that was oozing with maternal love yet combined with an intense yearning that said that she did not want to leave them.

Without batting an eyelid and maintaining an emotionless prosaic expression, Vineet's parting words to her were—"Leave it to God, He will do what is best for you."

In every man irrespective of his age or stature, a child within him always stays alive. Vineet at this moment could perceive the child in Mayan gradually surfacing and he had now without realising it taken on the role of an unrelenting father who was performing the duty of giving the right values to his child. He was also at the same time driving home the point that come what may, they would face it together. It is a foregone conclusion that beyond 'logic', the only eventuality left is one's 'Faith'. Drawing one final reassurance by holding tight Vineet's hand like one holding on to the last straw of hope, Mayan allowed her wheelchair to move on. Anjali and Suneet stood as silent observers overwhelmed with anxiety.

Every little while the nurse would come out of the 'OT' and update them about the progress in the operation theatre. "Everything is under control". "The surgery is going on". "All is well."

The needles of the clock hanging on the wall painfully crept on, as half an hour lumbered on to an hour. Anxiety was slowly beginning to build up again. Just then the 'OT' door opened and the nurse came and informed, "The surgery is over and has gone off successfully. She is being moved to the OT Care Ward. However, she will still take some time to regain consciousness. Once she gains consciousness, one member of the family can then meet her."

The family heaved a sigh of relief. They had overcome one hurdle successfully. "You meet her first," suggested Vineet to Anjali.

The OT Care Ward was a long open hall. Several patients had been detained there till they regained consciousness and then they would be sent to their respective wards. Some were on the drip, some on oxygen and others on both. Anjali's eyes were now anxiously searching for Mayan in that emotionally charged environment.

"She is over there," informed the nurse in an even tone. Anjali's pace automatically quickened to reach Mayan's bedside. Concern was plainly writ all across her face. Mayan's eyes were still closed, but she was letting off soft sighs of pain every little while. It was obvious that the effect of the anaesthesia was now gradually beginning to wear off as she was frequently alternating between gaining a little consciousness and then losing it. Sitting down next to her, Anjali began tenderly stroking Mayan's forehead. Mayan gradually opened her eyes. Blinking a couple of times in an effort to recognize her surroundings she softly uttered, "Lalli," the pet name by which Anjali was addressed by her immediate family. Relieved of all her suppressed fears she affectionately caressed Mayan's cheeks, "Are you feeling okay? Very shortly, they will allow us to take you to our room. Should I now call Vineet and Suneet?"

The nurse immediately intercepted, "Sorry ma'am, the chances of infection are very high here. The patients are getting unnecessarily disturbed. Very soon we will be shifting her to her ward; they can then meet her there."

"I understand," Anjali conceded.

However, a little while later the nurse returned to inform Anjali that she could call her brothers in to meet Mayan. Probably there was still some time left before they were planning to move Mayan into the ward. Dr. Anupam too, in the meantime, came down from the OT to check on Mayan's condition. He was very particular about taking due care and ensuring proper hygiene. He took off his shoes outside and entered after putting on a clean mask, gloves and a washed apron over his clothes. It was nice to observe that even Government hospitals were maintaining due hygiene and sanitation. Meanwhile, both the brothers Vineet and Suneet had come and met Mayan. After a brief gap, the attendant arrived informing, "Mataji is to be moved to the ward in the patients' lift." Immediately, everyone stood up and followed the stretcher moving along the corridor towards the lift.

The attendant stopped them, "You cannot enter this lift, please take the steps down to the ward." All three quickly rushed towards the steps to reach the ward. By the time they could reach, Mayan had already reached the ward. The nurse, accompanied by a couple of ward boys, had entered the room with their shoes on.

"Here they go tutoring others about hygiene but look at them, they are blatantly flouting their own set norms. Look, how they have dirtied the room's floor," an agitated Anjali muttered in an undertone.

"Don't overreact, we will have it cleaned again. But if they should overhear they might react and then we might land up with an unnecessary situation on our hands," Vineet reprimanded Anjali gently.

To follow the policy of playing it cool and following the Dale Carnegie method was the smart way of ensuring a support system in the hospital.

By now Mayan had fully regained consciousness. The nurse in charge came with the prescription slip that had Dr. Anupam's prescribed medication enlisted. She asked for the medicines to be purchased immediately so that they could begin administering the medicines as per the doctor's directives. Dr. Anupam too came on a round and called Vineet aside to update him on how matters stood for the present.

"The cancer is spreading very rapidly. It is of an aggressive nature. Within a week, it has spread quite quickly. I have, in total, removed 19 nodes already from axilla. For the time being, I have cleaned out the cancer thoroughly and Mataji is now fine. She will have to continue with the painkillers for sometime. However, extreme care needs to be taken to avoid infection. Do not encourage people to meet her."

"Yes, Doctor Sahib we will take all due precautions," Vineet confirmed. Anjali and Suneet were also listening to the doctor's directions.

"Once the biopsy report comes, we will decide the further course of action. In the meantime, I would advise you to contact the cancer department and meet the Head of the Department of Radiotherapy, Dr. Preetam. And yes, also contact the heart specialist as she needs to be under his care as well, as her heart condition too needs very careful monitoring," Dr. Anupam further advised.

"Yes doctor," both Vineet and Anjali answered in unison.

Dr. Anupam further went on to instruct, "As the lymph nodes have been removed, therefore the drainage system will now be impacted. A tube will have to be put to drain the fluid separately. I will give necessary instructions on my prescription and you can acquire the apparatus from a medical store. Along with the tube they will also give a measuring cup. You will need to carefully measure the drainage every day and meticulously maintain a record.

"We will need to maintain this record for how long doctor," Vineet enquired.

"You will have to do so till the drainage has reduced to less than 50 ml per day. With time, the body will on its own make an alternate course. Oh yes, during this period in order to prevent the backward flow of the liquid in the arm, you will have to get an arm glove (a special kind of a sock) tailored according to her size. I will arrange for the supplier to meet you. You will have to ensure that 'Mataji' keeps it on. However, at regular intervals the arm will need to be massaged moving from her wrist up towards the shoulder and never vice versa," the doctor further cautioned.

Vineet nodded his head, "We will do as you instruct, Sir."

Then turning his attention to the patient Dr. Anupam bent down towards Mayan in a reassuring tone, "Mataji, may I now take your leave, you will be perfectly fine in a few days," saying so he left the room while giving last minute instructions on his way out to the head nurse on duty.

An operation is over in no time but the recovery period is very exacting and long. As Mayan recovered slowly the realization now began to hit her that one of her breasts had been operated upon and removed. It is only natural for a woman to take considerable time to come to terms with this unfortunate fact glaring her in the face.

Mayan was no exception. In some of her weak moments, her facial expressions would reveal the hurt, the pain that she was undergoing. Nevertheless, she was always quick to camouflage those emotions. In the initial postoperative days, an ugly deep red seepage continued to drain from the operated section of her weakened body. The sight itself was terrifying. It was heart wrenching for her loved ones to see her suffer so. It was almost as if her blood was being gradually sapped out of her body.

Gradually the wounds started hurting with a sudden sharp wrenching pain at frequent intervals. To relieve the pain it was not considered wise to administer strong and frequent painkillers, as there was the possibility of them affecting the kidneys adversely. As it is, Mayan was already a chronic patient of a multitude of ailments. In Agra, that had been her hometown for so many years, Dr. Vitul had all along been their family doctor. He was familiar with Mayan's medical history. Vineet regularly consulted him with regard to Mayan's medical issues.

"I will strongly advise you against giving her 'Voveran', instead let her take a 'Crocin' six hourly. It should do the needful," Dr. Vitul strongly objected.

"But here the doctors are advising otherwise."

"This will only result in increasing her acidity and that will in turn result in gas formation. It will only increase her trauma. Mere antacids will also not be effective," Dr. Vitul reasserted over the phone.

And as it turned out just plain and simple, 'Crocin' did the trick. It was truly no less than a miracle.

The pain had now reduced considerably and then Mayan's fortitude made up for the rest. Three to four days had elapsed. The fresh wounds were now gradually being covered with a protective crust. The healing process had finally set in.

Now it was time to start her radiotherapy sessions. The following morning at nine o'clock all left with Mayan. The doctor was scheduled to arrive at 9.30 a.m. They wanted to avoid, as much as was possible, having to make Mayan wait. It is customary to have a long wait outside the doctor's room for consultation. It was as if the whole world was suffering from this dreaded disease. The sights that were revealed before their eyes as they approached the doctor's cabin were heart wrenching. Fear was now beginning to set in as they entered the hospital. If one let one's eyes wander across to the patients occupying the sides of the corridors, it further confirmed one's brewing fears. The earlier fears were now once again beginning to resurface. Deformed figures, dark blemished skin patches that now concealed the probably once pleasing facial features, all deepened the suppressed insecurities. One particular patient suffering from mouth cancer now presented such an ugly, pathetic, heart wrenching sight that even Vineet for a second stood rooted to his spot numb with fear as the magnitude of the terrible possibilities began to sink in, sending a chilling shiver down his spine. What terrible deformity! Instead of a mouth, there was now a huge gaping hole.

The waiting crowds that had gathered since the wee hours of the morning outside the head of the Radiotherapy Department, Dr. Preetam, were gradually beginning to reach uncontrollable proportions. 'Cancer' is symbolic of 'death', that is the common belief amongst the laymen. All those accompanying their suffering patients carried on their faces evident expressions of helplessness and dejection. All around, you could see them trying to pacify their depressed, afflicted relatives. One's attachment to life, a feeling of responsibility towards one's near and dear ones and the urge to meet the expectations of society, all collectively act as the driving force in one's reactions towards life and its taxing complexities.

Today is a world of mobile phones and their presence amidst us often provides extremely humorous situations. You will at times come across such situations where the overpowering, varied and modulated noises created by the presence of these princely mobile phones render speechless even the boards that hang along the corridors announcing 'Kindly maintain silence', "Please keep quiet". We often brazenly overlook these boards proudly announcing our illiterate misfortune.

Meanwhile, Dr. Preetam arrived promptly at 9.30 a.m. Recognising Vineet he warmly greeted him. Then noticing Mayan he commented, "You really shouldn't have bothered her, you could have just come with the reports."

"We have brought all the reports, doctor," Vineet informed the doctor.

Having invited them to accompany him into his clinic, the doctor entered his room. All three immediately followed him in, realizing that arriving early had been a wise decision. It had resulted in the doctor noticing them. It was fortunate, as they had thereby skipped the long never-ending train of human chain outside his chamber.

"So, the report says ER positive and PR negative. 'Her-2-neu' is positive. It is two plus..." Dr. Preetam gurgitated on the case for a couple of minutes and then proceeded to think aloud, "Doing radiotherapy could pose a problem in Mataji's case as her heart may not take the stress, being already weak. Though the test reports and their parameters still offer a slim possibility, I suggest you to get a detailed IHC (Immuno-histrochemistry profile) done. If then 'Her-2-neu' should read 'three plus', we could consider going in for a 'targeted therapy'. It will entail a course of 16 injections, once each month, for 16 months and it also has no apparent side effects."

"We will go by your advice, doctor sahib," Vineet agreed expressing his belief in the doctor's directions.

"In the meanwhile I am prescribing a medicine that she will need to take-one tablet a day," Dr. Preetam informed, simultaneously penning the details on the prescription slip and then handed it over to Vineet.

Vineet then proceeded to brief Dr. Anupam about the outcome of the meeting with Dr. Preetam. Dr. Anupam expressed his reservations. "Look I believe radiotherapy needs to be done, but then Dr. Preetam is the specialist in this line and we will go by his decision. You may collect the 'plates' from the lab. Also, please get a 'fish test' and 'IHP' done at 'Leela Pathology'. The report will take two weeks to come so I feel it makes sense to take Mataji home in the meanwhile. Being in a weakened state, chances of infection are higher here within the hospital premises. However, all due care must be taken at home. Precautions should be carefully enforced," the doctor warned. "I am enlisting all the details to help guide you. She should be constantly wearing the sock on her arm and a regular massage of the arm is to be done as earlier instructed. Carefully monitor the drainage; once the drainage reduces to 50 ml, the tube should be removed. Moreover, I am always available round the clock over the phone. Keep in regular touch," was Dr. Anupam's parting shot.

Mayan stayed in the hospital for the next three days as several other tests were completed. The reports of the heart test, bone density test and some other related tests had come in during this time. The 'heart ejection ratio' was around 60-65. However, the fish test report would take some more time to come and the course of the treatment would be finalized only after that. The foremost dilemma in their mind now was that during that intermittent period the nodes should not multiply again. The earlier records were pointing towards that possibility as within the last three months the nodes had multiplied from one to nineteen. The concerned doctor was strongly against administering radiotherapy. There was an obvious conflict of views between the doctors. Was Dr. Preetam taking the right call? Was he well qualified to decide? These different reservations were now arising in one's mind.

The pros and cons of the treatment were being continually discussed by the well-meaning relatives and friends also. A big question mark was gradually forming regarding the rationality of the administration of radiotherapy. What if it had an immediate and damaging impact on her heart? All were a little nonplussed regarding the right decision. What is the right one or were they endangering Mayan further? Then as is always the outcome of all perplexing issues, finally, believing in the Almighty they came to the consensus that what the doctor had decided had to be right. Therefore, the decision was taken to go ahead with his advice.

□

4

The unpredictable side of life can sometimes be very exasperating. This exacting side of life can sometimes completely dishearten a simple uncomplicated soul. But Mayan was an exception to this rule. Her belief in her 'Isht' was so complete that it was not easy to shake it and she firmly believed that unless God so ordained nothing could be moved. So by accepting the highs and lows in her life she maintained her composure and remained stoically unaffected, at peace with herself and continued to modestly accept it as her destiny.

Life is a continuous process of unravelling new chapters in one's life where every man gets to experience the different stages of his life with a novel perception. Mayan's life too had taught her to accept life in its changing colours. Some may disapprove of Mayan's return to her home so early but if you were to perceive it from her personal angle, she was relieved and happy to be back on her home terrain again. In fact why only Mayan, anybody else in similar circumstances would experience the same relief. After all the hospital is not exactly a spirit lifting experience, is it?

Typically, on arrival, Mayan's opening comment was, "Now you just wait and watch me. I will soon be on the road to complete recovery and then I will resume my 'Satsang'." Every day after that, she would religiously convince herself and those around her of the same. After escaping the harassing struggle in the hospital every man looks for some peace, some relief in their home's welcome surroundings. Mayan too was no exception. But the actual struggle begins when the so called social and customary perceptions result in the constant flow of visitors, each in his or her own way expressing their so called wholesome and well meaning concern regarding the patient's well being. After all, it would be pointed out as a sinful and inexcusable lapse on their part that society would not easily forgive if they were not to make that gesture of visiting the ailing patient and expressing their apologetic concern. To prevent the consequent flow of infection around the patient's already weakened low state of immunity becomes an insurmountable task in itself. Some of the more practical and the sensible well-wishers understand and appreciate the request to avoid meeting the patient. Others consider it a personal insult and react, simply refusing to understand the vulnerability of the situation. For Vineet, it was the case of once bitten twice shy. With a recent very damaging interaction when a gentleman in his attempt to show his genuine concern and authorized knowledge of Mayan's ailment had released such a gruesome and ugly picture of a cancer patient's plight that Mayan had then regressed into deep depression. So now, Vineet had firmly given standing directions that no visitors were to be allowed to go beyond the outside lounge area. Each member of the immediate family was now religiously following the instructions. Some visitors did create an awkward situation when they insisted on their right to atleast a glimpse of Mayan as they had taken the trouble to travel long distances just to see her. The genuine, truly involved, however were very understanding of the vulnerability of her present condition and were satisfied just sitting outside and making enquiries about her present situation without making a melodrama of what they could or had done. They quietly stood by the family, contributing to the required services and the necessary support system.

"Oh, If only I had been aware of the gravity of her situation, if only someone had taken the trouble to inform us earlier, we would have certainly contributed to the help required but anyway do let us know in the future if we can be of any help," was the assurance that was often rendered by a majority of the so called close relatives and associates.

A week had passed and Mayan's wounds had visibly begun to now heal, so the dressing was also being done after longer intervals. In fact, the 'fish test' report too had come, so they requested Dr. Preetam to give some time for consultation to ensure the further course of action. He graciously made himself available the following day itself. "Her-2-neu is 3- plus. In this case, hormonal therapy will be effective. We will need to administer a 'three weekly injection' for a period of one year. That should cure her of this malignancy," Dr. Preetam declared.

"Sir, Dr. Anupam seemed to feel that radiotherapy may..." one of Mayan's family members mildly interjected.

Dr. Preetam's reaction was immediate and extremely sharp. "What is the need to repeat the same thing again? Am I merely responsible for administering the medicine alone? To ensure the efficacy of the administered medication I need to first assess the condition of the concerned patient. After all, she is a heart patient. To perform radiotherapy immediately above the heart area on the left breast could be extremely risky. Yes, if it had not been a case of 'Her-2-neu positive' then I would have considered taking the risk."

"Yes sir, we completely agree with your line of action," the family member realizing the delicacy of the situation immediately retracted his stance and shook his head vigorously in agreement.

"What is the need to bring up the same issue again and again? After all Doctor Sahib knows what is best for her.

Anyway, that is a rather drastic measure, which will also result in severe discoloration of the skin. If hormonal therapy as per the doctor's advice is doing the needful then what is the need to question the course of action. Obviously this is what God also wishes for her," another relative standing nearby gently reprimanded. In the meanwhile the doctor had directed his attention on Mayan, "Mataji, you are a very brave lady and that clearly reflects on your face. Please trust me. This treatment will last only for an year and you will find that by the end of it the cancer would have been completely eradicated. It is a tried and tested therapy. I have already tried this treatment very successfully on several other cancer patients. It is a targeted therapy specifically meant for curing breast cancer. I assure you the results will be extremely positive."

To repose complete trust in one's doctor is a powerful recourse for a patient. Besides, Mayan reposed complete belief in her God. So taking it as the will of her 'Lord', she gave her consent, "look if the doctor is advising this course of action with so much conviction then I feel we should just go along with his advice. I am sure everything will eventually be fine".

They commenced the treatment immediately. However, after administering the very first 'Herceptin' injection, other complications began to set in. To locate her veins to administer the injection was becoming difficult, so the doctor next advised that a chemoport was needed to be put to simplify the situation as then the medicine could be conveniently injected through it without having to prick the skin repeatedly. But to put the 'chemoport', Mayan had to be again admitted in the hospital for 2 days. It was to be set in the body through a minor process of surgery. But this time Mayan played difficult and threw a fit like a little child playing hard to comply, "You people need to now spare me from any further surgery. Why don't you just try harder, you will find my veins."

Dr. Anupam was approached again. He cajoled Mayan like a father patiently bearing with his daughter's unreasonable tantrums, "Mataji, this port will come in very handy later on as well. Please take my advice and let us go ahead with it. Anyway, it is not a complicated procedure at all. It will be over and done with even before you realize."

His convincing style finally set Mayan's fears at rest and she conceded. The surgery was arranged and the chemoport put. It is a standard process to wait it out for 72 hours before it becomes functional. Dr. Preetam advised that they needed to wait for another day. "The next injection is due. We will apply it via the chemoport, so that the system to be followed for the forthcoming injection can be regularized." But, as is often typical of life, you overcome one hurdle and immediately the next presents itself. So was it with Mayan's treatment and her ailment. In fact, it seemed as if God had decided that she had to cross more than a normal share of hurdles. Though the injection was being administered, the Chemoport turned out to be dysfunctional. Immediately, she was back in the OT- this time for a stretch of three long hours, the doctor struggled to activate the port but to no avail. Then they contacted the manufacturer of the port and the port was finally replaced. The replaced port worked for a short interim period but it was not going to be easy to ensure its success. Mayan resignedly had now begun to wonder what more sufferings were still in store for her.

The doctor was himself bemused, "You know I have till date placed more than a 100 chemoports and never faced any problem with their functioning. It also comes from a very reputed firm." The assistant standing besides him too confirmed the honesty of the statement.

Meanwhile they had also contacted Dr. Vitul, who advised that they needed to take a second opinion. "I have a close friend belonging to Agra, working there in the same hospital. If you should feel the need, you could take a second opinion from him," he said handing over the contact number of Dr. Saral. After consulting Dr. Saral, Vineet and Suneet made some fresh discoveries. "I believe in following the conventional path. To deviate from the classic protocol automatically has an increased element of risk involved. If the treatment works, then we are lucky, otherwise, it can present fresh complications. On the other hand, pursuing the classic mode of treatment may entail a longer duration to take effect but the risk element is certainly reduced considerably," Dr. Saral advised.

"So, according to your assessment the course of treatment being followed is not advisable," Vineet anxiously enquired.

"Oh no, not at all, this is not what I am trying to say. I have also read a lot of material regarding this course of medication. But, these medicines are still at the 'trial and test' stage. Lot of fresh pharmaceutical companies have now entered into this field. The disease being a life threatening one, the medicines are extremely overpriced and the profit margins very high. Since they are covering a very critical ailment, these medicines have a defined market. And then to top it all the doctors get a very heavy commission on the same," Dr. Saral revealed without mincing any words.

A stunned Vineet reacted, "Are you really trying to tell us that even in this field, such dirty games are rampant. I would have thought that atleast they would spare..."

Cutting short Vineet's loud thinking, Dr. Saral elaborated, "That is the greatest tragedy of today's life style. People will go to any extent in their pursuit to accumulate wealth, even put the lives of others at risk. 'Certifications' today are now freely available for a price."

What then followed was pindrop silence for the next few minutes.

Alarming thoughts were now racing through a perturbed Vineet's mind. Could they have fallen into a similar trap? Were they in their effort to save Mayan actually further endangering Mayan's chances of survival?

Realizing that his words had made a deep indent in Vineet's mind, Dr. Saral now tried to reassure him "Look that is not exactly what I had meant. After all Dr. Preetam is a very seasoned specialist in his field. There is no denying that he is the Head of his Department and has a lot of experience behind him. There is actually no harm in trying out the hormonal therapy".

Vineet and Suneet left for home. However, Vineet was now not at peace, and so, he went on to consult several other doctors. Greed was not an unknown sphere for him. How greed could motivate the best and the most capable to deviate from the path of honesty and integrity was not something new for Vincet. He had faced similar situations during the course of his professional life. How, without it pinching their conscience in the least, dealers would blatantly go on to supply sub-quality bulletproof jackets and bullets to our soldiers. Those soldiers who were fighting on our country's borders to ensure our security were thus cold bloodedly pushed to their early grave. When their conscience had remained undeterred then what was unusual about such similar depraved souls to be sending the already suffering to their grave! To expect compassion on the part of those companies and their representatives was a far-fetched and impractical expectation. But the fact that the doctors too, the direct representatives of God, the so-called saviours, on whom mankind bestowed complete faith, were also in this money making racket was actually a bitter pill difficult for Vineet to swallow. Yes, he was not unaware of how the doctors received a commission in the test reports and tests provided by the pathology labs but to take commission where a life threatening disease was involved was difficult for him to fathom. There is an age old Hindu saying that even the demon spares one's own house. No, this could not be possible. Both the doctors, Dr. Preetam and Dr. Anupam were renowned doctors; they could not be party to such underhand, inhuman dealings. It simply seemed to be too far-fetched an allegation. Turmoil now flooded Vineet's thoughts. All kinds of negativity now ran amuck his thoughts but then he waved them aside. After all, one cannot give up faith in humanity. One has to lay one's trust in someone and particularly in the doctor with whom you have entrusted the life of one who is dearer than one's own life.

Mayan's hormonal treatment lasted for one year. The doctor took great care and precaution. They maintained a continuous watch on the heart ejection factor and the bone density issues. Time lapsed without any perceived complications. Other treatments were also administered smoothly. In carefully monitored doses, Mayan was given the hormonal therapy wherever she happened to be at that prescribed time, if in Delhi with her son, or in Agra the facility was duly provided. A sense of peace had now finally begun to set in their hearts with the belief gaining ground that the cancer was well on its way to complete recovery and the worst was now behind them. After one year had lapsed Dr. Preetam had another 'PET' done and no trace of cancer was detected. The doctors along with Mayan's kith and kin were now convinced that the cancer was well under control as the medicine was obviously having a very positive effect. The doctor confirmed that Mayan was safe for at-least the next five years and they would need to review her case now only after five years.

But destiny had other plans for Mayan. The unpredictability of one's life can sometimes be frustrating and very difficult to comprehend. In fact, it can take a serious toll even on one's firm belief in the 'Preserver'. Nevertheless, Mayan's faith remained unshaken. She happily accepted the ups and downs in her life as her God's wish. Yet, what she believed was now the end of her quota of suffering and trauma was actually only an intermission. The next phase of her suffering was soon to commence.

Mayan, who was well read in the field of the holy discourses given by the sages and the saints, always believed that one should welcome one's suffering with open arms, as suffering was the first stepping-stone that would take us closer to our 'Lord'. Moreover, it was this strong faith in her Deity that helped her cross so many hurdles that had so far come her way.

To define her deference towards the Lord and the Almighty she often narrated an engaging anecdote. "Once a master enquired of his servant, "What is your name?"

"Whatever you feel fit to call me by, my master," the servant replied without a moment's consideration. The master further enquired, "What would you like to wear?"

"I will dress as you deem fit, master," pat came the servant's modest reply.

The master further enquired, "What would you like to eat?"

With complete servitude in his tone the servant spoke, "Whatever you will feed me master."

Perplexed the master further dug in, "And where would you stay?"

"Wherever you deem fit to keep me, master," the servant conceded without hesitation. Such was Mayan's dedication to the Almighty.

Finally, a month went past without any complications until one fine day Mayan once again felt some fresh lumps in her left breast. They consulted the local doctors immediately. They were advised that all the investigations should be repeated without losing any time. Again an FNAC test was done. Once again, cancer was confirmed. In the meanwhile, Vineet had been transferred to Lucknow. On hearing the news, he immediately took leave and rushed to take her to Delhi.

Fear and insecurity had gripped him again. What would be the outcome now? A month back, when he had visited Mayan at Agra everything had been just fine. In fact, the doctor had then put Mayan on oral medication, which she had been taking very religiously. Why the reoccurrence then?

Upheaval now followed in Vineet's core between his 'faith' and 'disbelief'. Helplessness was slowly housing itself in their midst. It was a night that stretched endlessly between desperate prayers and a seething sense of anger combined with intense frustration. It seemed to be a morning which came after a very exasperating wait. They needed to get to the hospital now, they needed to get to Dr. Preetam and enquire, "Sir – what happened to your assurance that for five years she would be safe?" Vineet was now close on the verge of a breakdown. However, he somehow kept his emotions in check as he realized that he needed to put up a brave front in front of an already visibly shaken and nervous Mayan. But a mother can always sense what her child is undergoing, however hard he may try to conceal his emotions. Without his having to say it, she had already understood his nervous and insecure state of mind. Trying hard to find solace in her Lord, she consoled Vineet, "'He' tries him the most, whom 'He' loves the most. To help us make penance, 'He' makes us suffer but his comforting hand always remains above us. 'He' does this to gradually detach us from our worldly existence. We cannot understand 'His' ways, so let it be as 'He' has wished it for us."

□

5

Each individual has to struggle alone to define one's destiny. One's crucifixion is one's only route to salvation. To detach oneself from one's personal bondages, and to crucify one's worldly bondages, is the only route to attain the final stage of purity. Then, one successfully evolves and becomes one with the 'Sublime'. Such were the thoughts now racing through Vineet's mind as he approached Mayan. Then, he gently bent down to murmur some tender reassurances in Mayan's ear.

To be forced into a situation where you are left with little option but to once again undergo that blood curdling situation where you are continually facing a life threatening situation of suffering the agonies of a disease like cancer is bound to send repeated shivers all the way down your spine. But then, what other option is left when faced with such a situation. Vineet and Mayan had to travel immediately to Delhi. As Vineet was no longer posted in Delhi, he had already given up his Delhi residential quarters to move to Lucknow. Now there was little option left but to move her into a guesthouse in Delhi. They put her up in the luxurious comforts of a VIP guesthouse but that did not in anyway mitigate their discomfort or add to their peace of mind. The guesthouse's staff was very prompt and supportive and the facilities offered were near ideal. Yet, these provided the mother and son duo no solace on that 'cold dispassionate' Delhi morning.

Everything around Vineet today appeared to be dull and so pointless. Mayan had finished her morning prayers and was now wanting to leave. "Vineet if you are ready, let us leave," Mayan anxiously reminded her son.

"There is still some time left to go. I have ordered some breakfast. Eat something and then we'll go." Vineet could sense an unusual sense of dullness that was overtaking him today.

"Is Suneet joining us directly at the hospital?"

"Yes, brother is reaching there directly, you know his house is closer to the hospital," Vineet clarified. Soon breakfast was served. Both picked at the food as if their appetite had been killed after being guilty of having committed a sacrilege and now not knowing how to make amends. They had just finished having breakfast when an old friend of Vineet, peeped through their door, without bothering to wait after a brief knock, "May I come in?" Both mother and son turned to look, "Arre, How did you come to know that we are here?" Vineet's incredulous expression said it all. "We always keep a very close tab on your movements my dear," came Hemant's good humoured repartee as he moved into the room accompanied with his wife, Malti who bent down to touch Mayan's feet to take her blessings. Malti gently rebuked, "Vineet bhaiya, even though you kept us in the dark but Jiji had informed us that probably you are in Delhi putting up at the Lajpat Nagar guesthouse. So we decided to try our luck."

"Oh! What a pleasant surprise," Vineet expressed his genuine pleasure.

Then taking Hemant aside, Vineet informed him of the latest adverse developments. In the meanwhile, Malti lending a supporting hand was slowly guiding Mayan towards the gate, as they were now already late in meeting the hospital deadline. "The two of you can follow us to the car," she reminded her husband and Vineet, thereby making her point that they needed to move now.

Hemant had already taken the day off in order to accompany Vineet to the hospital. But dissuading Hemant's intentions Vineet persisted, "What is the need to do so just now. I will let you know when the need arises."

"Well then you know best. We will do whatever suits you but we had come with the intention of being around to extend whatever possible help," Hemant drove home his point.

"No really, I'll let you know when the need arises," Vineet insisted.

"Please don't take it otherwise Vineet, but I just want to let you know that whatever I have is also yours. Presently there are Rs. 2 lakhs lying in my bank account. I have brought the cheque along. I am leaving Malti here with you to take care of aunty. I am also leaving the car with the driver here to use as and when required," Hemant stated his intentions.

Touched to the core by the genuineness of his friend, Vineet smiled indulgently, "Hemant, I know how goodhearted and genuine a friend I have in you. But seriously, right now I will manage. Since you have now allowed me the liberty, stay warned. If and when I should need anything, even if you should then resist, I will not spare you then but take it as my due right. After all, you have now given me the right to do so, is that not so?"

To define the relationship between Hemant and Vineet would not be possible. However, it would suffice to say that Hemant's father who had left for his heavenly abode only a few months back had always regarded Vineet as his own son.

Having already reached the car, Mayan asked the driver to honk to remind Vineet that they were running late. Vineet immediately bid goodbye to Hemant, rushed to the car and instructed the driver to take them to the hospital.

Fortunately, the road leading to the hospital via south extension was not crowded so they reached their destination well in time. Suneet was already there waiting for them. He waved to catch Vineet's attention. As the car drew to a halt, he hastened to hold Mayan in a tight reassuring embrace.

Then he went on to inform Vineet, "Dr. Preetam has just arrived and has gone to his chamber. Let us head straight there."

A wheelchair awaited Mayan. Seating her, a male nurse manoeuvred her wheelchair towards the doctor's chamber with Vineet and Suneet following them.

Suneet mumbled, "How the hell has this happened. Dad informed me last night. I could not sleep a wink after that."

"Some things are beyond our comprehension. Now whatever it is, we can only try our level best. The rest is best left in God's hands," Vineet resignedly consoled. Vineet had already informed Dr. Preetam. So, he was waiting for Mayan in his chamber. How genuine is a doctor's concern for his patient's well being and subsequent suffering is hard to define. However, if a senior doctor finds his case being spoilt, the adverse impact that it makes on his reputation is naturally a matter of immense concern to that doctor. This became apparent to the patient's associates in the next couple of hours.

How one's perception undergoes a complete change according to the changing scenario became glaringly apparent to both Vineet and Suneet today, as they crossed the same radiotherapy unit corridors. What had last time seemed an ugly and loathsome sight to them was today arousing emotions of abject helplessness and pain. The surrounding walls today appeared to be dark, threatening; their ugly stains were taking on the most torturous sight clearly reflecting the depth of the disillusionment and despair that was gradually setting in their psyche. Every cancer patient seemed to be anxiously awaiting his final release from the curse of this unbearable suffering. Now, as they approached Dr. Preetam's chamber, his assistant stepped out to inform Vineet that Dr. Preetam was at present attending to another patient so they could take a seat and would have to wait for their turn. In the meanwhile he went ahead to immediately make a phone call. Later on, they discovered that he had made the call to Dr. Anupam who had removed Mayan's breast and the nodes, to join in their consultation. This became apparent when they saw the doctor approaching them from the other end of the corridor. Then, together they entered Dr. Preetam's consultation chamber. Dr. Preetam stood up to greet Dr. Anupam.

"Let us proceed to the adjoining chamber. In the meantime, Mataji can wait here. Vineet please could you join us," Dr. Anupam acknowledging Dr. Preetam's welcome beckoned Vineet and Suneet.

"Of course, let us proceed to the adjoining room, it is vacant right now," Dr. Preetam confirmed and then proceeded to inform the other waiting line of patients that he would now be able to see them only on the following day.

The adjoining room was the retiring room for the senior doctors. On the arrival of the two senior consultants, the other junior doctors present there immediately rose and left the room.

The doctors then requested Vineet to produce Mayan's earlier records. Vineet had meticulously arranged the records under individual headings. Some of these files had already become rather bulky. Pathological reports, the heart's ECG and echocardiogram reports, bone density test report, papers related to the surgery, BP, sugar and so many such other papers were record wise all individually filed for easy access with proper detailed index. The doctors kept asking for and Vineet kept producing them without any delay.

Reiterating the details of the case and the records, Dr. Anupam could no longer hide his agony and now pointedly flung the accusation without mincing his words at Dr. Preetam, "I'm really sorry. But when I had sent her to you, if only you had agreed to administer radiation therapy, I can vouch that today the cancer would not have returned. This, when you are the Head of the Radiology Department."

"It is simple for you to make these judgemental calls. However, you are overlooking the then delicate condition of the patient. I still feel I was justified in giving her hormonal target therapy instead," Dr. Preetam defended in a belligerent tone.

"But I was the one who had done the surgery and had carefully removed each and every sign of the nodes. I had cleaned out the nodes completely. There wasn't even the remotest sign left of them and then inspite of that, if the case is botched, I feel morally responsible and challenged. Even then I will still go on and accept your stance," Dr. Anupam gave his consent but his tone obviously reflected otherwise. It was apparent for all around to realize that he was extremely exasperated at the other doctor's stubborn stance and at the unfortunate turn of events. Perceiving the rising tempers between the two doctors Vineet mildly intervened, "Sir, you are both seasoned doctors in your particular lines. Whatever has happened was probably destined. After all a doctor merely treats but the cure eventually lies in the hands of our 'Creator.' So kindly forget about what has happened and why. Instead please advice on the course of action to be taken henceforth." Vineet was fully aware that this blame game, if allowed to go on, would only complicate the situation. Anyway, a doctor's intention is not to take the life of his patient. Inspite of the best efforts if the case should get complicated then it was not fair to blame the concerned doctor. In fact, the need of the hour now was to come to terms with it and accept it as the patient's destiny and God's ordinance.

Then, at this critical point of time, to consider changing the doctor also may not be a wise step as where was the guarantee that the next doctor's 'modus operandi' would definitely bear positive results.

"But Mataji's health is too frail to attempt a secondary surgery," Dr. Anupam now gave his verdict.

"I realize the gravity of her plight. Probably, to give her a low dose of chemotherapy may help. But before we proceed on that course of action, I will advise you to get a biopsy test done on the fresh nodes, so that we are able to make some headway in solving the riddle behind the reoccurrence of these cancer nodes," Mr. Preetam advised.

Dr. Anupam nodded his head and advised Vineet to take Mayan immediately to the minor OT. A Biopsy was done and the sample sent for assessment.

"As soon as the biopsy report comes, which should in any case not take more than two days, please come along with it to me immediately," Dr. Preetam gave clear instructions.

After a lapse of two days, the biopsy report came and Dr. Preetam was in for a mild shock.

"Oh my God, this report shows both the factors as negative. The ER that was earlier positive is also negative now," Dr. Preetam announced.

"But the report is accurate. I had called and enquired about the result from the lab earlier. The sample has been tested twice. The previous report had also been sent. This report is correct," Dr. Anupam confirmed.

"But how did you know, the report has just come in," Dr. Preetam inquired.

"I have been especially concerned about this case, I had requested the lab incharge, so he reported the result to me on the phone itself earlier," Dr. Anupam clarified.

"Yes, once in a while one does get emotional about a case. In fact, after a certain age how the cancer may progress is difficult to determine. With both the factors being negative, it clearly indicates that this cancer is very aggressive in nature and will spread to the other parts of the body quickly," Dr. Preetam put forth his views.

"Then what course of action do you suggest," enquired a concerned Dr. Anupam.

"We will need to administer a strong chemo course. How much her system will be able to tolerate is what we will need to define. I'll immediately have some tests done," suggested Dr. Preetam.

Vineet, a silent observer for quite sometime now intervened, "I can see you are both trying your level best but if only you could clearly indicate that what should be our expectations now, sir?"

"I am prescribing some tests and the chemotherapy that we are considering," Dr. Preetam elaborated.

"If the test reports so indicate, I will suggest that you ensure that she undergoes the first chemo session right away, here itself. Then it will be administered after a regular gap of 15 days each. All in all we need to give her six doses of chemotherapy."

The tests were conducted and then the first dose of chemotherapy administered. There are not many side effects that are apparent after a hormonal therapy is given, but chemo results in several of them. The patient starts losing hair, even the facial appearance undergoes a visible change, and that obviously affects the patient psychologically. To top it all, the immunity goes down considerably, increasing the chances of the patient catching the infections present in the surroundings. At such a time, those responsible for the patient need to take very special care and the required measures. Dr. Preetam explained all these issues at length. After a careful briefing, he even took the trouble to inform

Vineet that when they needed to come back for the next dose. However, if they preferred to have the chemo given in Lucknow itself, he could introduce them to a local doctor, who would do the needful. He then went on to give Vineet the details, the name and address of the concerned doctor in Lucknow.

The sudden turn of events had made them wary of the after-effects that might follow the new suggested line of treatment. To confirm doubly that the now advised treatment was the right one, was the natural and expected reaction as one who is once bitten is twice shy. So Suneet flew down to Bombay to meet a super specialist in this line, who was attached to the famous Bombay Cancer Institute. The doctor made himself available since they had taken a prior appointment. He carefully ran through the entire case from the very beginning to the present and then declared, "In the present circumstances the line of treatment is correct. We would have also followed the same course of action. However, the patient's condition needs some special care and precautions. If you should so desire you could fly her down here. Though the line of treatment would remain the same so you can even continue with the treatment in Lucknow. It is as per your convenience."

Further, he elaborated, "There are some latest technologies that have been recently developed and are available with us. I suggest you let the chemotherapy be given to her in Delhi. If as the situation develops and radiotherapy is needed, we now have the equipment to give the treatment through 'a low dose radiation' which will ensure that her heart is not adversely affected."

"Doctor Sahib, do you visit Delhi often? If yes, it would be convenient to bring mother down to Delhi for you to see her. Her next chemo session is due in Lucknow. If you should so suggest we will bring her to Bombay," Suneet enquired from the doctor.

"I think I have an examination session lined up at Benaras University in the next 15 days. If possible your brother could bring your mother there and I will examine her," the doctor counter suggested.

Suneet then returned to Delhi and after a detailed consideration, the family reached a consensus that it was wise to continue with Dr. Preetam's treatment only.

The second course of chemo was administered in Lucknow the following day. Dr. Preetam had clearly defined the protocol to be followed.

The family was introduced to the Lucknow specialist Dr. Shalabh, who was to now monitor Mayan's case locally. He came across as a keen and seasoned professional. He was very particular in ensuring that both his staff and the patient's attendants were compassionate, careful and gentle in their dealings with the patient. He was obviously well versed with the psychology of a cancer patient. The very first day he briefed Vineet, "Before we give Mataji 'chemo' we need to first conduct a blood test to determine the 'RBC, WBC and the platelets count.' Chemo results in reducing them considerably in the patient. In addition, the sodium and potassium ratio tends to go haywire too. Considering Mataji's medical history, the difficulties she may suffer from any medicine that is given to her would have an immediate impact on her health. Then we have to take particular care of her heart condition. So you need to meet a heart specialist and keep him duly informed about her condition. I will personally brief the doctor. Similarly, a general physician should be constantly monitoring her sugar levels and her blood pressure. Another possibility that is highly likely to complicate her problems is the possibility of her suffering from fever and other such complications due to her falling immunity. So please make sure that you maintain a record of all our contact numbers in case any unforeseen complication should arise."

After carefully considering some other related problems he further advised, "The other side effect of chemo-therapy will be frequent headaches, vomiting, nausea, giddiness, gas formation, an upset tummy and a whuzzy feeling in the head. You must have a list of some medicines that would provide immediate relief to her if any of these symptoms should surface. However, you must ensure that they are given to her only SOS, that is, as and when required only. Now the most vital advice that I am about to give you is that kindly bring a change in your own life style, eating pattern etc. according to that of the patient's needs. She will need a specific diet. Many life style changes will now be essential to ensure her well-being. Therefore, in order to make sure that she does not feel deprived you will need to reduce sour, spicy, rich and acidic food from your diet as well. That will prevent any unnecessary cravings or a sense of deprivation in her."

"Sir, the point has been registered and we will ensure that we do the needful," Vineet assured the doctor.

"No, but it doesn't stop here, there is a lot more that you will need to do. We will try to minimize Mataji's stay in the hospital. As her immunity decreases, her chances of catching an infection will increase in the same proportion. As you know that a hospital is a hotbed for infections so she will be safer at home, provided all necessary measures be taken to keep the house environment safe and properly sanitized. The right of entry into Mataji's room will be curtailed and only those who are attending to her personal needs should have access to her room. Before dealing with her, hands should be carefully washed and disinfected. On entering her room, a fresh apron should be put on over the clothes and a mask put on to prevent passing on of infection. Footwear worn inside the house should be kept separate. Her clothing should also be carefully disinfected (her bedding, towels, etc.) and changed every day religiously, mopping of the floor with phenyle in the house and particularly her room should be disinfected at least 2-3 times."

"Yes sir, I am aware of these as Dr. Preetam too had cautioned us about these precautions," Vineet nodded in consent.

"I'm repeatedly stressing on these issues because these are vital to her health and her chances of recovery. Do not encourage visitors at all, as this could be a major threat to her health. If it should be essential to interact then place the speaker of the phone at a good distance and then let her exchange a few words, and that is it. However, this is a very tricky situation as she should under no circumstances be made to feel that she is helpless and a burden because that could have a very negative impact on her psychology. Therefore, it is the first and foremost duty of those attending to her that they ensure that she remains in a positive and a jovial frame of mind. This is most essential," and with these warnings Dr. Shalabh finally concluded his dictates.

"Whom should we contact regarding her diet, doctor?" Vineet further enquired.

"Yes, I'm informing Dr. Reddy about that. The dietician will approach you and hand over her diet plan. We will need to keep her diabetes issue also in our mind when deciding her diet chart. 'Chemo' will adversely affect her insulin so kindly also ensure that you consult Dr. Sharat in this regard."

"As you advise sir," so saying Vineet collected all the papers and took Dr. Shalabh's leave.

As and when chemo was given, it brought with it new and more painful experiences. Vineet was now finding it difficult to handle it all alone so he requested Anjali to come and share the responsibility with him. She immediately came and stayed on each day for quite sometime. The changes that are ushered in after chemo are rather frightening. The patient writhes in pain and remains continuously restless.

Similar was Mayan's plight. So much so that often just to provide her some temporary respite her body had to be covered with cold packs. That would give her some moments of respite from her constant anguish. Days and nights had now intermingled and lost their significance. Realizing that both Vineet and Anjali were fast reaching a breaking point, well meaning friends and relatives now chipped in and offered to take turns to come and assist in her care and to look after her.

Chemo results in very marked fluctuations in the insulin level. One needs to monitor the blood sugar levels at least 2 to 3 times a day and keep the doctor duly informed. Initially, her sugar levels were far exceeding the ideal levels but then later they dipped far below the permitted levels. So they had to ensure that there was some sugar kept within her reach. In fact, once they had to give her sugar syrup quickly to revive her from a coma like state and bring her back to consciousness.

At such critical times, it is imperative to ensure that those who are genuinely attached to the patient and care about the patient's wellbeing, should be around them. Those who come only to make a point, do not really bother to take any due care and precaution to ensure the safety of the patient. If such farcical people surround the patient, then his life is truly endangered. Vineet did not want to take any such chances so he had already appointed well-trained professional nurses round the clock to look after Mayan. After all, what is money's worth when your own mother's life is at stake? Though if we were only to look around in these modern, self-centred times, people find taking care of their parents an unnecessary burden. And if these parents should turn sickly then this burden becomes even more unmanageable for the children. Moreover, so many today then simply dump their old parents in old age homes and wash their hands off any further responsibility towards them by merely sending their monthly upkeep expenses. If others are unsuccessful in doing so, they simply proceed to push out the belonging of their parents on to the terrace or outside their main door and then throw morsels of food at them as one would feed a stray dog. The poor helpless parents, having nowhere left to go, tolerate the humiliation at the hands of those very children who were once the pride of their lives, the apple of their eyes and the very essence of their existence. However, such was not the case with Mayan. Her children left no stone unturned to ensure she received the best treatment and support.

Chemo plays out its own complex games. Since they had been already forewarned they were ready to control the situation if and when it should arise. Dr. Shalabh had pre-warned them that the sodium and potassium levels in Mayan's body would fall. And it did. In fact, they dropped so low that she had to be immediately admitted in the 'heart care centre' for treatment. That helped overcome the crisis. Timely treatment was given and she managed to recover after a mild heart attack. She was then onwards regularly given potassium pouches. Becosule capsules were emptied out and refilled with salt powder. She was given this twice a day for 2-3 days until the salts in the body reached the necessary levels.

Now the next complication to tackle was the swelling that had spread through Mayan's body, thanks to the imbalances in the 'thyroid' and 'insulin' levels. Vineet and the other relatives were now reaching at their wits end as to how to balance the different levels in her body that needed to be carefully monitored and maintained. The medication given to control the swelling had resulted in disturbing the sodium levels in the body. There was a new doctor called in for a new ailment every day. Which medication would send her system reeling was now becoming an unsolved riddle. What side effect would then ensue was becoming a cause of constant worry and concern. It was now becoming more and more apparent that they needed to have an efficient general physician who could accurately ascertain and assess all her parameters and draw a quick and correct conclusion to follow the necessary course of action and medication.

The constant suffering and excruciating agony was now also beginning to take a heavy toll on Mayan's morale. It was gradually wearing away her confidence and ability to bear pain.

"What terrible blasphemy have I committed to be at the receiving end of such suffering," Mayan let off a deep sigh of frustration and helplessness. Vineet and Anjali were now accepting her fast growing negative state of mind. They had never seen her give up on anything. She had always been a born fighter.

"Ma, you have dedicated your entire life serving the holy saints and devoting all your energies to selflessly taking care of your family. You have only worked for the good of all those around you," Vineet consoled his mother.

"May be it is the deeds of my earlier birth that I have to bear these sufferings now."

"True, but one can never tell. Yes, now that you mention the effect of our deeds of our previous birth, that reminds me of an incident in Mahabharata related to Bhishma Pitamah that explains the Karma theory," Vineet reiterated.

"What is that?" Anjali questioned.

"You see, when Bhishma Pitamah was lying on his bed of arrows and undergoing unbearable, excruciating pain, he had posed a similar question to Krishna. Lord Krishna had then explained the reason behind it," Vineet elaborated.

"Oh yes, I have heard it too. 'Pitamah' had then responded that he clearly remembered the life that he had lead in his past hundred births. As far as he could remember he had not committed any action, even remotely close, to have to undergo this unbearable suffering of having to lie on that bed of arrows. It was then that Lord Krishna reminded him of his 101st birth, because of which he now deserved to suffer this destiny," Anjali further elaborated.

"You are right, but it would be best if we did not go into the nitty-gritty of the repercussion of our actions in our previous births," Vineet suggested.

"I understand what you are trying to say but one's heart refuses to concede to such logic," Mayan explained.

Long after the discussion was over, Vineet still could not stop reflecting along that train of thought. 101 births back, an act that Bhishma Pitamah had done where he had wounded and thrown a poisonous snake into a thorny bush and left it there to die, its life slowly seeping out of its body. This suffering that Bhishma Pitamah was now undergoing was actually his act of penance to repay that 'Karma'. According to Hindu philosophy, even the Gods had to repay for their acts of omission or commission in accordance with the gravity of its repercussion whilst in their human form.

Following this train of thought Vineet gradually sunk deeper and deeper into his thoughts, realizing that each human being had to make his own cosmic assertions, undergo his own crucifixion, finally unload all his worldly connections, and sacrifice his dearest possessions and bonds. The final bonding with the Almighty was possible only after we successfully severe all human bonds. Then the human form that emerges is truly pure and holy. Vineet bent down and whispered into Mayan's ears, "You need to consider this as God's blessings being showered on you. Rather than considering this physical suffering of your human form, take it as the route that is slowly taking you to the state where you will become one with the 'Creator.' It is your source of the final release from all human bondages that will leave you in a pure and sublime state. Ma, you only taught us to 'accept God's Prasad' as God's blessings being showered upon us and not enjoy it merely for its taste and a means of satiating our sweet platter, else it would merely add calories to our body. The same theory is now applicable to human bodily suffering. So consider it and accept this pain as 'God's endowment' upon you and submit to His blessings with the same spirit and dedication. Overlook the suffering, realize that when the body weakens, intellect fails and the ability to reason wanes and then it is, one's 'faith' and 'faith' alone that provides one with the sublime strength and the power to endure," Vineet was frankly expressing himself, a little taken aback that how he had come to perceive life in this context and philosophy. Had he finally matured to a level where he could think along these lines, a thought process so pure and divine, a state that uplifted you beyond worldly constraints and bonds and made you realize the true meaning and purpose of 'birth and death'. Without realizing when and how, Vineet suddenly felt that the very purpose of 'life' and 'faith' had finally been disclosed to him which is the only actual 'path' that man was meant to tread upon.

A few years back Vineet's life had undergone jolting upheavals such that had shaken him out of his mental state of complacency. Life was not and should never be taken for granted. In a recent episode, an explosion had taken place right under his vehicle as they had driven past. How he had survived this blast still remained an unexplained miracle. Mayan's reaction then had been, "who can tell what the Lord has ordained. Even negativity hides within it a positivity and 'His' blessings. Look for and acknowledge 'His' blessings and 'His' benevolent aura that actually protects you and helps you to move on in life. Find a new purpose, look for fresh urgings. After all, you are my son, and most certainly not a weakling. Struggle, overcome and never give up your everlasting belief in 'Our Creator'."

One had never felt the need to preach and motivate a woman like her earlier, a woman who had all along been so strong and spirited in her approach to life. An old episode that Mayan very often narrated was a standing evidence of what had been the true crux of her life and existence. One night it had so happened that an emergency had arisen as the milk in their house had finished. Therefore, she promptly left at 11 o'clock at night to walk four kms from the house to a shop to fetch milk. There was not a soul to be seen along the dark yawning road that led to the shop. Every emerging figure in the dark appeared to be a threat to her safety. With several tales of how travellers had been looted in such dark and lonesome streets continuously racing through her thoughts she quickened her pace to reach the milk vendor's shop. Several questionable looking characters who were outside the shop turned to stare. In that dark night, holding desperately on to a tall, copper glass, her face covered with her sari's 'pallu' she softly asked, "Bhaiya, could you please give me ¼ kilo of milk." Someone from the crowd passed a lewd comment that further quickened the pounding of her heart. Tightly grasping the glass of milk close to her, she quickly turned to retrace her steps back to her house. An increasing sense of insecurity was now taking hold of her with every step. The shadows in the dark were growing longer and more threatening as she bravely carried on. Once in a while she would turn to ensure that she was not being followed. Beads of perspiration had begun to form on her forehead with her heart pounding fast. Further quickening her pace she started praying desperately to her Guruji, her 'Lord and Master', to come to her rescue. Suddenly, she sensed a strange calm settling on her as she sensed the presence of her Guruji walking by her side. She now felt secure as he led her on safely to her doorstep. When she turned to thank him, he was nowhere to be seen as though he had already melted in the darkness of that night. Now, Vineet reminded her of this miraculous experience of her past, in an effort to reinforce in her the belief that it is one's 'Faith' and Faith alone that can make you raise yourself to a level where you can experience the 'Supernatural and the Sublime', right here on this earth itself.

This reminiscence suddenly brought a blissful brilliance on Mayan's facial features. Her face now lit up like a brilliant lamp that successfully dissolves the darkness spread around. Not one to easily let go of a chance, Vineet took a little dig at her, "you know what Ma, you don't really pay worthwhile attention to the discourses given by our 'Maharaj'. That is why though in each of his discourse he repeatedly insists on the cleansing of the 'Ghat,' that is, the 'inner self', you interpret it as an instruction simply to clean the 'Ghar', that means the house and so you go about scrupulously cleaning the house with the broom instead. Seriously Ma!" Mayan joined in these lighter moments and his tomfoolery that now surfaced ever so rarely. She broke into a peel of giggles and playfully ribbed Vineet back affectionately. "Yeah, of course you are the only literate one amongst us. You, my brilliant son, my genius, now you take the responsibility of grasping the true meaning of the teachings and then explain them to me. What is the need for me to wreck my brains then; after all, I have you to do it for me, don't I?"

Vineet knew that he had managed to achieve the desired success in his mission. Even if it was temporarily, he had still managed to bring back the old Mayan. The Mayan who had always accepted everything very sportingly and as a challenge in her life!

□

6

In an effort to ensure Mayan's recovery, the family had also taken to other alternate healing therapies. Some benefit must have come to her through these. If only they had started them right at the onset of the disease, probably the results may have been more definite. However, the reason for that not happening earlier was either they had never considered these therapies as of any relevance or may be they had even shirked the responsibility off by shifting it on to other's shoulders as each had probably been a tide too busy handling their own personal affairs.

Finding that the results via the standard medical science (allopathic medication) were not turning out to be very conclusive, Vineet and the rest of the family now considered opting for 'alternate therapy' as well. There was a time when the Indian Ayurvedic mode of treatment was considered very evolved and effective. After carrying out careful investigations and enquiries, they discovered that actually there were several possibilities of curing Cancer in this stream of medical treatment as well. Though, it was equally essential to verify the authenticity and the safety of their application. They met a renowned specialist in Jaipur who had discovered a herbal remedy for cancer after several years of dedicated research. After going through a detailed breakup of all the herbs that had gone into making this medicine Vineet also had their properties and their safety checked at the 'Central Drug Research Institute' at Lucknow. The deductions drawn stated that all these herbs helped to raise the general immunity of the patient along with increasing the alkaline base that is present in the body. After being somewhat convinced regarding the efficacy of this course of medication the brothers then went ahead to meet the concerned Ayurvedic doctor in Jaipur. The doctor revealed several realistic facts to them. "I have used these herbs to make a suitable combination to treat cancer, all based on my personal experience. Although, they may not give any immediate and miraculous results but they will most certainly build the immunity of the body gradually and decrease the acidic content of the body. Cancer cells grow and prosper when they are provided with an acidic environment. Given that, they then begin to progress and slowly eat into the body finally leaving it hollow. My strategy to cure the patient is to gradually reduce the acidic content in the body and increase its alkaline content, thereby ensuring that the cancer cells are not provided with a conducive environment to grow and multiply any further. By providing a hostile environment around these cells and at the same time increasing the immunity levels of the body it will gradually kill the already present cancer cells and cure the patient. If you should wish, you can most certainly give it to your patient. After observing the success rate in several such patients, I have now patented this course of medication and am now recommending it for the suffering patients."

Accurately assessing the still continuing indecisiveness clearly writ on Vineet's face, the doctor further asserted, cementing his case, "I am not in favour of chemotherapy. In fact, I would very strongly advise you against it. The logic behind this is very simple. You are welcome to assess it on your own too. If some dacoits should enter a village and then intermingle with the villagers present there in order to avoid being identified by the police, then, should the police line up all those present in the village along with the villagers and shoot them all in order to ensure that the dacoits are killed. What about the poor hapless and innocent villagers then? Would you agree that it is a wise step to take? Also, what if it merely results in killing most of the good innocent villagers and not the dacoits. Then what would you do?" The doctor put across his point on such sound and concrete ground that Vineet was left with little choice but to begin to question the authenticity and credibility of administering 'chemotherapy'. After all, there was very sound logic in the doctor's argument.

Anjali's daughter who was studying abroad also went ahead to do a lot of research on the internet on her own accord and forwarded to them a book related to cancer. In fact, it provided some very useful information based on some detailed research conducted at the 'John Hopkins Institute', advising and giving precedence to some alternate therapies over and above 'chemotherapy'. They advised introducing some natural foods in the patient's diet to build up the immune system. In fact, they had gone to the extent of suggesting that surgery, radiation and chemotherapy were responsible for increasing the chances of the cancer cells spreading to the other unaffected parts and organs of the patient's body. They also were in obvious favour of ensuring the alkaline content in the patient's body. Milk, sugar, tea, coffee, meat, etc. were in the prohibited list of foods as they encouraged the toxic content in the system, thereby encouraging the growth of cancer cells. The opinion of several other specialists of diverse streams was also considered. All in all, the basic deductions drawn were that fresh vegetables, sprouted cereal, dry fruits and fresh fruits needed to be given to increase the alkaline content in the patient's body. They insisted that fresh fruits and vegetable juices were advisable, as they would provide the enzymes that would help to fight off the 'cancer.' Another fact that was discovered was that food, if heated beyond 40°C would result in the useful enzymes in the food being destroyed. All these came as fresh useful information.

While scrutinizing the details about the possible remedies they came across several already successful examples, resulting from the intake of herbs and alternate forms of medication. Unprecedented benefits had been observed after the use of natural product such as 'beriberi,' 'blueberries', acai berries and asparagus. Now their extracts were available in the market in the form of tablets that could be taken regularly and would most certainly benefit the patient. The extract of 'wheat germ' when given regularly also had considerable positive effect.

Then 'essiac-tea' and its consumption was also known to have a beneficial effect. Much literature was now made available regarding this unique concoction, though records of 100% of its proof of efficacy are in all truthfulness still not available. You are advised to mix and then refrigerate it like a tea mix, to be had thrice or four times a day. Even the use of the leaves of the tulsi herb is also advocated for such patients.

All these diverse herbs and medication were given to Mayan at regular intervals and they must have borne some positive results but probably they were introduced a little too late to control Mayan's cancer. It will also always remain undefined that if this course of treatment had been introduced in the very early stages of Mayan's cancer, then probably it would have made a more definite impact on the eradication of her disease.

"Consuming stale leftovers and eating a substantial quantity of pickles also increases the acidic content, thereby increasing the chances of cancer's acceleration. We really need to put an immediate stop to these," Anjali too gave her personal opinion. "And not just these, but all these preservative added products that we are bringing into the house will have a similar result," she further insisted.

"Further research in this area has revealed that asparagus is a potent remedy too. It contains a certain protein, 'histones' and 'glutathione', an anti-oxidant that are extremely useful ingredients. Fresh green sticks of asparagus are also available in the market, their juice can be conveniently extracted and refrigerated and then administered to the patients regularly – 4 teaspoonfuls both morning and evening for a period of at least 3-4 months to achieve definite results," this advice came from another well-intentioned quarter.

Cancer does not grow overnight in the body. So by the intake of the correct 'foods' a substantial resistance can be developed in the human body. Turmeric, blue berries, strawberries, green tea, soyabean, grapes, garlic, cabbage, broccoli, oranges and lemon should be introduced in one's daily diet. Gradually the family was learning these vital lessons but unfortunately a little too late. If only this knowledge had come to them at an earlier stage, the scenario could have been very different. However, for the future and probably for a lifetime, they had now learnt this lesson.

In the present circumstances, the family was now applying the due, diligent and feasible control measures. Of course, offering their prayers to their Deity and keeping their fingers crossed were the only two other alternatives left. One now had little option but to put in the best available to them in their effort to save Mayan, then to simply wait, watch and indeed pray.

□

7

It is certainly not advisable to leave one's patient totally in the care of the hospital staff. To provide the family's emotional support is so necessary to boost the patient to fight against the ailment successfully. Neither is it wise to unnecessarily crowd around the patient as that may expose the patient who is already having a lowered state of immunity to further infection. Besides, there are other patients around as well. In such a state of affairs, it becomes essential to avoid flouting the necessary rules and regulations as well as the ethical code of conduct set by the doctor.

In the meanwhile, the Mumbai Cancer Institute specialist happened to be visiting Benaras. Vineet and his sister Archana immediately left with Mayan for Varanasi. The doctor carefully examined Mayan. He very scrupulously scrutinized the various aspects of her present condition and then concluded that the proposed line of treatment was satisfactory as per the various parameters of the present state of the disease.

Unfortunately, another complication was to set in. The chemoport that was earlier placed, was now gradually developing an abscess around it and could result in spreading the infection. The doctor advised its immediate removal. He also suggested that after completing the present course of chemotherapy they should take her to Mumbai where they would be able to administer the 'radiation therapy' without it having any side effect on her heart. This was the most advanced machine that was now available to them.

After leaving the doctor, Mayan expressed the wish to meet her local relatives in Benaras. "Vineet, there are some of my village relatives living in Varanasi. Since we are here, let us visit them."

"Now, where and how have these relatives suddenly materialised? You have never mentioned them before," Vineet queried.

"I haven't met them for quite some time. My brother's second daughter is wedded to his younger brother. Let us go and meet them. I really want to, now that we are here. He is of a very sweet and likeable disposition and he has been like a brother to me. God knows if I will ever get to meet him later", Mayan insisted.

"Oh in that case he will be my mama (uncle) too. Okay, let us add another 'mama' to the already never exhausting line of our mamas," Vineet reacted typically with his tongue in cheek humour.

They then proceeded to the house of this latest addition to their family. Mama welcomed them with open arms and in his Marwari dialect, "Arre 'Baiji!' What a pleasant surprise! I am so overjoyed that I feel dancing like a peahen." Mayan gave a 'see I told you so' look to Vineet, as they both exchanged indulgent smiles.

Archana too had quietly followed them inside. She was a mute listener to their conversation. They stayed on for a while and then headed back for Lucknow.

The doctor in Benaras had clearly advised, "Mataji's cancer is aggressive by nature. It has the tendency to spread fast. How far mere preventive treatment will be able to control it and for how long one really cannot tell. Had this treatment been started earlier then probably it would have had a more definite result. However, there is no harm in continuing with it as it will only help and not harm her. However, if 'chemo' was to be stopped then it could result in the nodes immediately multiplying in both size and numbers. Then they may reach a point where they may even burst leaving behind huge gaping wounds." The picture that he presented was indeed both gory and frightening.

This revelation now left the family in a complete state of dilemma. What were they to do now? During this period of indecisiveness, the nodes began to grow and formed an abscess. After much deliberation the final consensus was that, a 'low dose' chemo should be continued. Mayan was again admitted to the hospital. Now 'chemo' had to be given to her only under the close supervision of the doctor. All her parameters had once again started to go haywire. Diabetes too had now taken a turn for the worse and become a cause for serious concern.

Nevertheless, Mayan continued to maintain her calm and for the benefit of her loved ones, a happy demeanour. She would look at all around her with indulgent affection. So much so that even the hospital staff attending to her developed a special regard for her in their hearts. All of Vineet's friends also came forward to help him to attend to Mayan. This was indeed invaluable support for Vineet. If you have to stay on with your patient in the hospital for a long duration then this form of support is really needed to ensure the proper looking after of one's patient within the hospital premises. Leaving the patient alone in such a state is the most harmful step that one can take to undermine the patient's confidence and the will to fight against the ailment. So you really need to take due care and at the same time safeguard the patient against exposure to any form of infection.

Now the 'chemoport' was removed as the area surrounding it and the right breast was becoming visibly inflamed with an abscess gradually developing around it. The infection had made serious inroads and now was fast becoming difficult to control. To top it all, the 'blood culture' report too was proving to be inconclusive since 'chemotherapy' was being administered. Therefore, they were not being able to decide the 'antibiotic' and its dose that would curb the spreading infection. Mayan had now started running low grade fever. This constant low-grade fever was giving rise to other uncertainties and doubts. Why was the fever not going? Could the 'low immunity' be resulting in tuberculosis as was often found to be the case in patients with lowered immunity? Now the entire test related to this possibility was done but to no real avail. The doctors were still not able to draw any clear-cut conclusion.

The next 'Chemo' was now administered minus the port. The nodes began to subside and reduce visibly. Dr. Shalabh expressed some satisfaction in this regard. However, post the 'chemo session', the blood reports became very erratic and were showing a blood composition count that was rather disturbing.

"Considering her present condition, I do not see the possibility of her being able to endure the next chemo. We have only 15 days available to us and how far the situation will improve is still difficult to assess. Atleast for the next 10 days the chemo will result in further dropping of her blood count. From now on, we need to get her 'blood test' done every second day. Please ensure that you keep an oxygen cylinder handy in the house itself. Keep yourself ready for an emergency drill," Dr. Shalabh did not now feel the need to mince words. The relatives needed to be alive to the situation on hand.

"Doctor, I have already taken these preventive measures and am keeping the necessary arrangements ready. I had actually taken note of it when you were advising another patient's relative the other day," Vineet confirmed.

Ten days had elapsed, but there seemed to be little improvement in Mayan's health. Then another five days went by but Mayan was still very frail and by no means fit to being able to take the next '.chemo' session.

"Now, you need to take a call on this. Really, even by the farthest stretch of my imagination, I cannot say that she will be able to endure the next 'chemotherapy'. It is quite possible that the forthcoming days will prove to be her last. Else she may pull along for the next 4-5 months before the cancer reaches its terminal stage," taking Vineet aside, Dr. Shalabh plainly put the present situation before the son.

It is not possible, particularly for a son, or any emotionally connected relative to take this call. It is like being in the precarious position of finding oneself sandwiched between a deep well on one side and a cliff edge on the other. Vineet had already seen a couple of cases of relatives of some of his acquaintances who had returned after having taken a prolonged and complete course of treatment in renowned cancer hospitals both in India and abroad. Yet they had not succeeded in fighting successfully against this dreaded disease and had passed away in the next one or two years. In fact, one of Vineet's own batch-mate, a very senior officer in the Government of India had undergone treatment for breast cancer in the USA. It had been followed by surgery, then radiation etc. but finally it had come to naught. Another senior officer's wife who had been undergoing chemotherapy to cure cancer had also lost the battle and died.

Bayaji was at that time looking after Mayan in Lucknow. Vineet considered her opinion too. She was devastated and broke down as tears rolled down her aged wrinkled cheeks. Besides being a close relative, she and Mayan had been close confidantes and the closest of friends too. Sitting across the small round table, facing each other in the living room, both sat mute looking deep into each other's eyes for some possible answers, for some ray of hope that would help instil some iota of confidence in them and some clarity of the road they were to pursue. But, for that moment, even the brilliance of the 100 watt bulb that was lit right above their heads was only succeeding in spreading the darkness of the final night fall. The walls surrounding them were now loudly proclaiming only dense desolation and defeat.

"Lala, I think you are right. Do not go in for 'Chemo'. What is destined will be, let us now leave it to fate. This way she may be around us at least for a few more days. But, yes I feel there is no need to inform 'kakaji' or anybody else of this development, so let us keep it to ourselves," Bayaji advised in a barely audible voice.

"I agree with you. I should not tell father about this development but I do need to consult Suneet and Anjali about it. After all, they have an equal right to decide," was Vineet's assessment of the situation.

"It is your final decision, I will leave it to you then," Bayaji conceded.

Both then went back to being mute spectators. For a while they continued to look long and hard at the threatening walls surrounding them. How that night slowly crept by was difficult to determine. Vineet could not sleep a wink that night. Harrowing thoughts kept passing through his mind. Peace and calm had quit his quarters for the time being. Finally, slowly composing his thoughts, Vineet reorganized himself. After offering his morning prayers, and asking his 'Isht' to endow his benevolence upon them, he prepared to leave. The hour of reckoning had now arrived. He had made the most difficult decision of his life and was now about to implement it too. To communicate it to the doctor was not the difficult part, but the impossible task was to disclose this information to Mayan. So far, they had always maintained an above board relationship where he had never hidden, twisted or minced words when communicating with her. Their relationship had always been above board and honest where nothing had been kept from each other. All along he had kept her truthfully informed about every little detail and change. But how do you tell your mother a truth so dark, so vile? How can you bare such a harsh reality to one's own mother? The mind dithered. Then, should he hide this fact, conceal it from her and change the norms that had been so far scrupulously maintained in their relationship? The question gnawed away at his insides but for how long, that was difficult to tell!

□

8

"I have not on my own accord said anything with regard to 'Mataji's' present condition. You have compelled me to confess inadvertently before you what the outcome in such cases generally is. However, I now expect you to maintain an optimistic outlook in the matter. To make any negative prediction goes strongly against my 'ethics' in my profession. Neither should a son follow such a course," Dr. Shalini clearly expressed her disapproval and unhappiness in the matter.

Vineet just could not muster up the courage to disclose the truth and gravity of the situation before Mayan. So concealing the truth Vineet attempted to console her saying, "The doctor has conducted a thorough check up. The nodes have clearly dissolved now and are no longer there anymore. Why don't you just go ahead and try to feel them for yourself?"

"Oh yes, last night I was trying to feel them too, but, couldn't trace them," the unsuspecting Mayan agreed. "Chemo is unnecessarily causing unrest and making you distraught, so the doctors have now decided to stop it. In fact, Dr. Shalabh has informed me that there is a very reputed doctor attached to the Bombay Cancer institute who practices here in Lucknow as well. She is Dr. Shalini. She specializes in the treatment of cancer and its medication. She has advised that instead of giving you the 'intravenous chemo', she will switch you to 'oral medication' only. That will do its job equally effectively. Just two tablets a day. That will also put an end to all those complications that follow when 'chemo' is given to you."

Mayan's face had lit up with joy. She had actually begun to dread this constant painful process, the constant day and night piercing of needles and its terrible after effects and the distraught state that this process resulted in. Honestly, she really had had her fill of chemotherapy. So now, it felt like she had been finally released from the shackles that had bound her for so long and prevented her from taking a free flight to enjoy the pleasures of inhaling in the fresh clean air of 'life'.

Mayan reacted, "That is the most wonderful news that you could have brought to me. Seek an appointment with that wonderful doctor at the earliest. I want to immediately meet her and start taking her medication. Then, I will regularly resume my 'Satsang' as well. I have not been able to attend it for so long. Even your father has been so lonely all this while staying all by himself." Believing every word that her son Vineet had uttered as the gospel truth, Mayan was now in the throes of a childlike enthusiasm. She began to make elaborate plans of all that she now planned to do. For a moment, Vineet felt like a culprit who had committed the most unforgivable, the most sacrilegious crime of deceiving her and actually taking advantage of her innocent and implicit trust in him. Then he rationalized it, consoling his own self, "At least, now as long as she is here amidst us she will live the way she wants to, happy, free and unchained."

Dr. Shalini was not a mere figment of Vineet's imagination. Dr. Shalabh had in fact mentioned to Vineet about her only a few days back. Therefore, it was not difficult to locate her whereabouts. Vineet managed to get an appointment from her for the following day itself. She was actually attached to a private hospital in Lucknow where she had been practicing for sometime.

There was a distinct charisma in Mayan's personality that always immediately won over whomsoever she happened to meet. Her elderly, uncomplicated, peaceful, honest, and affectionate demeanour unwittingly won the attention and affection of those around her. Moreover, if ever she had borne any grudges against any one, they had all now long dissolved along with the cancerous nodes that she had been undergoing treatment for. Along with her bodily cleansing process, her inner soul was undergoing the cleansing process as well. As soon as Mayan entered Dr. Shalini's chamber, she immediately set aside whatever she was then engaged in and quickly came forward to help Mayan to get up from the wheel chair. Then holding her for a second in a comforting, reassuring embrace almost as if a lost friend had finally met her after a long gap she led Mayan to the patient's chair. Vineet was intrigued by the similarity of several such instances during her treatment where whenever the going had gotten too complicated and they seemed to be reaching a dead-end, just then a new avenue would suddenly open, shining through the dark and would lead them on to a fresh course of action.

"Mataji, now please tell me how are you feeling? What can I do to help you?" Dr. Shalini opened the conversation between them.

"She is ..." Vineet tried to take the matter into his hands. Promptly, raising her palm to stop any further intervention for the present, "I would like to hear what Mataji has to say to me first. If you don't mind please, we will talk later," Dr. Shalini sharply interjected. Vineet immediately took the message that was conveyed. Simultaneously, Archana who had also accompanied them raised her finger to her lips warning him to keep quiet as well.

"If I should have a daughter like you, then illness will anyways not dare to come near me. I'm already beginning to feel normal," Mayan affectionately conveyed her feelings.

"That is exactly what I feel too. I wonder why these people are insisting that you are unwell. They have unnecessarily brought you here. You are as fit as a fiddle," Dr. Shalini confirmed.

"You have got it all wrong. My son has only brought me here to meet a wonderful daughter," Mayan caressingly directed her glance towards her son and corrected the doctor.

There was some truth in what Mayan had said considering Dr. Shalini's pleasing disposition and positive stance. The surroundings had now suddenly taken on an extremely cheerful and joyous cover. The most threatening and serious ailment would automatically be forced to make itself scarce in such positive surroundings.

The conversation however gradually moved on to a serious note between Vineet and the doctor, "I have already discussed her case with Dr. Shalabh. We will now administer oral chemo. A very effective medicine is now available. I am prescribing it for her. It should keep her cancer in check. The rest that you need to ensure is that she gets proper nutrition in her food. Her food should be monitored well. And of course keep her happy and well attended to."

Vineet directed Archana to move along with Mayan towards the awaiting car in the portico outside while he noted down the details of her prescription. The real purpose was to ensure that Mayan did not remain within hearing reach of the conversation that he now wanted to take up with Dr. Shalini. As soon as they left, Vineet humbly put forth his request, "Doctor I am well aware that you are an expert in your field and I will follow your instructions sincerely to the very 'T'. But I would be grateful if you could now please tell me about the true extent of the spread of this disease and if there are any chances of her recovery at all."

"Look my job is to treat the patient to the best of my ability. I am against declaring any 'negative assessment' with regard to my patients. It goes against my code of ethics."

"I understand, Ma'am, and I truly appreciate your values. Yet, if you could kindly let me have a broad idea about how it generally turns out in such cases," Vineet insisted.

"If you are so insistent on knowing the actual situation then I give her at the most three months. After that, the nodes will gradually form into an abscess and the pain will begin to intensify. Then the only option left will be to give her pain killers in order to relieve her pain somewhat. Once these become ineffective we will have to switch her to morphine. As for the rest, we are helpless. We then just wait and watch till the patient breathes her last."

"What you are saying is that you give her time only till this December or may be January?"

Dr. Shalini now reacted, "I have said nothing of the kind regarding Mataji in particular. You have compelled me to let you know what generally happens to patients with a similar history. However, you need to maintain an optimistic approach in her case. To provide a 'negative prediction' goes against my code of ethics. And a son should certainly not follow such an approach in dealing with his mother." The doctor now looked visibly perturbed.

Assessing the sensitivity of the moment, Vineet quickly arose and collected his papers. Then directing an apologetic glance towards the doctor took leave.

"All the best, God willing everything will be fine. If the need arises, I can visit Mataji at home to look her up. She is a very strong lady. All will be well," Dr. Shalini looked up from whatever she was noting down and gave Vineet a final parting reassurance.

They returned home. After offering his prayers to God Vineet sat down next to her and advised Mayan, "Devote more of your time praying and seeking the Lord's blessings. That alone can add to your peace of mind."

"Hmm," Mayan nodded.

"Now don't you go about sermonising? Ma knows it all," Archana teased Vineet. "Okay, whatever you say, Madam 'High and Mighty'. I humbly submit that I was in the wrong. But please...." Vineet had had a trying day and was in no mood for any further light hearted banter.

Archana left for her house informing Vineet, "I have already received 3-4 phone calls from home so I will have to leave for now but I'll be back in the evening."

After Archana left Vineet and Mayan continued to sit together, discussing various issues for quite sometime. "To tell the truth I am no longer able to meditate for long. All kinds of distracting thoughts keep racing through my mind nowadays. I really wonder how you manage it," Mayan enquired of Vineet.

"I'm no authority on this but it is just that I religiously abide by the 5 principles that I feel make a difference. I submit myself completely to the 'Lord' keeping in mind these 5 dictums," Vineet humbly admitted.

"Let me know them too," Mayan inquired of her son.

"But then how can I dare to guide you? After all, you are the one who has had the good fortune of staying under the guidance and care of our sages," Vineet commented.

"I have not really been exposed to the techniques they dictate of pursuing the path that leads to the Lord. But yes, I have been lucky to have been allowed to stay in their vicinity, serve them, clean their living quarters and cook for the saints as well," Mother humbly revealed.

"But then that is the true service to God," Vineet looking deep into his mother's eyes reassured.

"Look, don't try to digress from the issue on hand," Mayan was now not willing to let go of the issue so easily.

"Okay if I must, I will humbly attempt to explain it to you. It is nowhere near to being a sermon because I am in all honesty no authority on the subject," Vineet acceded hesitatingly.

"Yes, I am aware of that. Yet I am all ears for them," and saying that Mayan closed her eyes giving all her attention to what was to follow.

Then Vineet carefully unravelled to her the crux of each of those five principles that he felt would eventually help her to amalgamate with the 'Creator'. "If you merely give them a peripheral hearing they would be of little consequence. But if they were to be absorbed intrinsically then there is really no end to their significance in directing the path one should trace through the course of one's earthly existence. First and foremost, to humbly acknowledge His presence, praying to him "Oh! Lord, my Supreme Father you are the all-powerful. You and you alone exist and there is nothing beyond or besides you. Second, my faith, my belief lies in you and you alone. There is no faith beyond you, my Father. Third, I submit myself in totality to your Sublime Self. You and only you can purify my soul. I handover my person completely to 'you' to do with me as you deem fit, my Lord and master. If you should decide to change my physical entity and form, I will happily accept it and gratefully acknowledge that only Your wish shall prevail. Fourth, I express my desire and want for you and you alone. There is no wish, no longing beyond my desire to become one with you my Creator and lastly, whatever the state, form or plight You deem fit to keep me in, will give me complete happiness and satisfaction, as it is Your wish and You have defined that destiny for me. I will humbly accept it in all humility and absolute submission," Vineet was going on speaking in an expressionless tone while Mayan was listening with rapt attention, totally lost to the world.

Vineet continued in the same monotone, "All this while as I pray to the Lord I try and focus my complete attention at the focal point located between my eyes. Following the different precepts of 'Pranayam' that help me to regulate my breath and then to move to the higher 'echelons' of sublimity simultaneously remembering and praying to the 'Creator' above all else. Slowly, I move further and gradually blend with my 'intrinsic' self. Sometimes my concentration may break and then follows a deluge of conflicting thoughts and emotions that begin to threaten to take over. It is then that I resume my effort, going back into the initial mode of piety where I attempt to refocus on these five principles, putting in another fresh attempt to rediscover my 'Lord and Master'." "I think I understand what you are trying to tell me. Now, let me try it too. But you may need to repeatedly reinforce this sentiment and this passion in me to finally hand myself completely into God's hands," Mayan's tone had a fresh resurge of hope in it now.

"Hmm that is fine. However, first I myself need to achieve success in my own effort. Only then, can I become an authority and guide you. Maybe a collective effort on our part may get us some success," Vineet reassured Mayan.

He had realized that this might be a good means of keeping Mayan both distracted and sufficiently busy. One of saint Kabir's hymns was an all time favourite with Mayan. She would 'hum' it often with complete devotion. Their whole family actually were the followers of the 'Sant Mat' and saint Kabir was their first and foremost sage. Vineet now started singing that 'shabad' written by Kabir. Mayan immediately joined in an attempt to sing along even in her present weakened physical state:

"O my true Benefactor,
the reservoir of sheer Holiness,

enlighten me with your 'Benign Presence'!
As bereft of your gracious 'Aura',
I survive in a state of constant unrest.
Sans you, I have been reduced to ignominy,
and a perpetual state of distress has now overtaken me.
I pine relentlessly for your manifestation-
within me.
I crave for just a passing view of your magnificence,
my sincere utterances for you should now bear fruit,
as I render myself,
in complete submission,
at your Holy feet!!"
(Original verses at page 181)

They sang along, being carried with the flow of their arousing emotions. Tears began to slowly roll down Mayan's cheeks, wetting them with her conflicting emotions, sometimes drawing her towards the intensity of the words of the rendition, sometimes being swayed with the pangs of yearning that were leaving her feelings devotionally entrenched.

□

9

Mayan had made her kitchen the family's cementing factor, the force that had bonded the entire family together keeping each in close proximity with the other. Unfortunately, in today's world, the lack of this is obvious and in fact is successively becoming more and more apparent in the modern generation. So today, you will find the modern generation catering only to their own individual palate and taste, dining separately at varying hours according to their own personal convenience and certainly not as a close-knit family unit that sits and shares its meals together. This generation now blatantly disregards the age-old adage 'the family that eats together stays together.' In fact, times have really changed today, so even the kitchen fires remain cold most of the times as food is generally 'ordered in'. Thus, meals that 'bounded a family' with those bonds of love, nurturing and care is no longer applicable in today's world.

Mayan's health had lately been showing some signs of improvement. She had even taken to going for short walks in the nearby park both in the morning and evening. Gradually, she was going back to her old normal life's routine. Forgetting the sufferings that she had undergone in the past she was now living under the temporary umbrella of her belief that she could once again revert to her old life routine. Going with the flow of her prevailing mood, Vineet too decided to go ahead and arrange a grand celebration where all their family and friends would join in to partake in her happiness with no holds barred. Soon the opportunity presented itself.

Archana's younger son Anuj had stayed with Vineet while he was studying in Delhi. Anuj held his uncle in very high esteem and Vineet was also very attached to Anuj and cared deeply for him. Initially Anuj grudged the discipline enforced upon him by Vineet who believed in maintaining a strict disciplined lifestyle and expected the same from Anuj. However, very soon they struck a balance and a very strong bond developed between the two. The same nephew was now getting married and his in-laws too happened to reside in Lucknow. The girl he was set to marry had also studied in Delhi and Vineet had been her local guardian. She too was extremely attached to Vineet and regarded him akin to her own father. Therefore, Vineet's joy knew no bounds at this auspicious bonding. In fact, Mayan too was very attached to the two and she had spoilt these kids no end during her stay in Vineet's house in Delhi. The two children were also very fond of Mayan. They would spend the whole day hovering around Mayan, their 'Nani', that is, maternal grandmother.

Their wedding ceremonies actually commenced with a celebration in Vineet's own house. All their friends, relatives and acquaintances were invited to join in. A very grand and sumptuous spread was laid out for the guests. Every detail in the arrangements was carried out under Mayan's personal guidance and instructions. Mayan was now in a carefree and happy frame of mind. She got ready for the occasion wearing one of her best saris. It had been quite sometime when she had last dressed up like this for any occasion. With the aid of her walking stick and 'Chottu', a boy who remained in her service round the clock, she went about personally supervising and ensuring that all the arrangements were as per her instructions.

The guests began to arrive. Vineet made it a point to introduce each guest to Mayan. She blessed them warmly. That day she was in very high spirits. She was ecstatic and spreading happiness all around her. In fact it was after a long time that she had actually enjoyed a hearty meal to her heart's content. She had even arranged for the appropriate gifts with which she blessed Archana, her son and her daughter-in-law to be.

Vineet had also arranged for a short cultural programme wherein two well-known vocalists belonging to a local troupe of Lucknow entertained the gathering by putting up an engrossing performance.

It being a cold winter evening, the lawn was dotted with temporary bonfires to warm the surroundings. In the golden light of these, the winter flowers which were in full bloom growing all along the periphery of the lawn were radiating a unique brilliance that was reflected in varied hues. All the guests had come in their best and colourful attires and were adding to the cheer that spread all around.

It had been ages since Mayan had experienced such bliss and happiness. She cherished every moment of it. Vineet's efforts had successfully borne fruit. Getting emotional, she expressed her wish to Vineet, "I wish your father was here too with us, he would have been so happy." A Hindu married woman, born and brought up with firm traditional values will never feel complete unless she has her 'better half ' by her side sharing such special moments with her. She then went on to voice her wish to thank her Lord for giving her the opportunity to be a party to such happy moments. "Will these professional singers sing some holy hymns, a 'shabad' of Kabir on my request as well, Vineet?" "Why not," said Vineet. He then approached the troupe and enquired if they could sing the 'shabad' as was Mayan's wish. "Mataji, we will sing whatever you ask us to," replied the head vocalist.

"Then sing a 'shabad' of Kabir, the saint," requested Mayan.

The 'shabad' that they sang then had not been heard by most present there, yet it received more attention and appreciation from the crowd than even the unparalleled compositions by 'Amir Khusrau'. They went as:

"I am soaked to the core,
in your love, O my Deity!
I have need for no caution,
as I have found my final solace.
Those who suffer the pangs of separation-
from their beloved,
need wander;
my beloved now dwells right here within me,
my thirst is quenched and my wait is over.
In the throes of my love,
'Uncertainty' is now a thing of the past!'
Further says Kabir, "If you intend to tread-
along this precarious path,
then shed all the unnecessary load,
and go along carefree and burden free."
(Original verses at page 181)

The 'shabad' was a long one yet the duo sang it without refrain, again and again. The crowd cheered on just as appreciatively. The words found their interpretation and appreciation according to the level of the understanding and mood of those present. That night was followed by a week-long marriage celebrations. Mayan was present there throughout those ceremonies. One of the lunches served consisted exclusively of the Rajasthani platter. Hailing from Rajasthan, Mayan conveniently overlooked the doctor's orders and restrictions and savoured the flavour of each preparation, so much so that even Archana forgetting the thrill of her son's marriage for that moment happily commented to Vineet, "Did you notice Mayan, she looks so happy today, doesn't she?" "I was also thinking the same. In fact she had hurt herself this morning but she seems to have forgotten about it for the moment. I am ever so grateful to God," Vineet agreed.

One of Mayan's greatest sources of joy was to cook and serve food to not just her near and dear ones but to all and sundry who happened to come to her doorstep. In fact, she had often cooked lavish feasts single handedly. So amazing were her culinary abilities that she would cook simultaneously a multitude of dishes all on a burning gas, a kerosene stove, infact even a wood or the coal fire, dexterously using one to boil, to cook, to fry or roast at the same time, thereby proving her multi-tasking capabilities. This concept of multi-tasking was introduced much later in the computer world but she had been a robot fitted with computerised working abilities way back in time. She could put the right spice in the right proportion even with her eyes shut. In fact, this secret had made her successful in keeping all her family tightly bound together in a secure familial bond that could not be easily severed or broken. Once one had tasted food cooked by her cherishing hands one was then enslaved forever. She was also a master at making various pickles and this skill had won her the love and appreciation of many. The love reflected in the genuineness of her gestures made it impossible for anyone to refuse her requests. It was particularly her kitchen skills and her generous love that had bonded her entire family so closely. Unfortunately, this is what one finds often missing in today's world. Today, everybody likes to fanatically guard their privacy, the privacy of their time and also their choice of food. Different meal schedules are now maintained, different foods and very often, readymade foods are also ordered in. Thus, 'food' that once was a source of nurturing relationships, of cementing them and spreading love and solidarity has now become non-existent and a 'had been'.

□

10

"You have now arrived at the beginning of the final lap of life's race. This is a race that you have run wilfully and successfully right through the entire course of your life so far. Now is the time to gradually submit all worldly bondages in the care of 'He', who nurtures us all. You now need to completely with your heart and soul submerge yourself in 'Him', our 'Creator'. 'His' and only 'His' name should now resound in your ears and occupy your complete concentration. 'Death' should now cease to be of any consequence. It is the final hurdle that you still have to overcome to reach the culmination of your life's race and finally become one with our 'Definer', our 'Destiny maker', our God. And this is and will be the only meaningful and fulfilling step during the course of your entire existence so far" – was Vineet's constant submission to Mayan.

As the month of January approached, Mayan repeatedly expressed her wish to return to Agra and participate in the initializing 'Satsang' of the coming New Year. Eventually, giving in to her repeated urgencies and armed with all the necessary equipments and medications, she was brought back to Agra to once again unite with her long separated husband and her home. Dr. Vitul gave the reference of a very capable and competent local cancer specialist in Agra, who also happened to be his very close friend and colleague. The gentleman was running his private clinic in Agra, a very qualified and a grounded doctor who had also done a specialization course in cancer from the Mumbai Cancer Institute.

A month flew by comfortably without any untoward development.

But then oral chemo too has its own share of side effects. The skin of the limbs gradually begin to darken and thicken, turning somewhat gory to the sight, as it gradually turns rough with cracks surfacing slowly. The doctor sufficiently reinforced with his experience had already warned them and prescribed a special cream to treat this condition. It was now being applied at regular intervals throughout the day to relieve the condition. Besides this, 'Chemo', as is well known, makes its distinct impact on the efficiency and working of diverse body elements and organs. So, now a noticeable swelling could be seen in her entire body, it had begun to look disproportionate and the skin had developed an unnatural shine due to its stretching. A medicine had been introduced to control the swelling, but then it meant another additional deadly threat— the chances of sodium content suddenly dipping. Her blood pressure levels too had become unpredictable and the bones too, already weak and brittle, were further weakening. She had already suffered for quite some time with a chronic ailment of a stiff back and weak knees. Movement for her meant she had to exert and that caused heightened exertion on her already weak and ailing heart resulting in a sudden surge in her blood pressure. One of the after effects of this was that her head would spin. Thus, the chances of her losing control over her limbs had increased resulting in her chances of falling and hurting herself. A very typical symptom that she had was that stress would immediately result in enhanced gas formation in her stomach. Now despite the cancer medication, these

-health conditions had shown a marked deterioration. Things were gradually getting from bad to worse. In this present scenario, the only solution left was to arrange for a wheel chair in which she could be taken to attend the 'Satsang' sessions. The attendants were sternly instructed to take very great care to ensure her well being and comfort.

Pitaji was also doing his very best to contribute to her well being to the best of his ability considering his age and frail health. It was now that Vineet received official orders to proceed to London to undergo a month long training course. Following the orders Vineet had gone to Delhi to complete the necessary formalities required for foreign travel. It was then that he got a call informing that Mayan had suffered a paralytic stroke. Dropping everything like burning ember he rushed to her side. Suneet was already present there. After taking all the details from Suneet, Vineet followed it up with getting all the necessary investigations done and the required medication began. Unfortunately, despite all possible effort the left side of her body remained completely paralysed right till she breathed her last. So many pros and cons were considered and carefully investigated as to why the stroke had occured but no real conclusion could be reached. The damage was permanent. Any amount of justification or clarification now remained a futile exercise. Her suffering remained irrevocable. To understand another's predicament and extent of suffering is near impossible and this is what one realizes when faced with such a helpless predicament. We are all instruments, mere puppets in the larger than life game plan of the Creator of our world.

Vineet did not leave for London. He requested his seniors to cancel his training, as he needed to be beside his mother.

However, taking adequate care of Mayan was now becoming more and more difficult. Very soon, she had to be shifted to the hospital for a short duration and some new medication had now been introduced. But looking at her frail physique and low vitality, continuing to keep her in the hospital was now becoming more of a threat to her life. In her present weakened state to pick up an infection in the hospital environment was a very genuine and likely threat, which could result in further complicating her case. Therefore, corresponding facilities and arrangements were made available at home by the sons - a folding bed, oxygen cylinders, an I.V. stand, professional nursing staff, complete sanitizing of her room etc. were all arranged for. Suneet's wife had come and was ensuring that complete care was enforced in Mayan's best possible interest.

Yet gradually, Mayan's condition was deteriorating and every consecutive day the situation was becoming more and more precarious. Her daily regime too had to undergo frequent changes, as things were now most unpredictable. There was an imperative need for somebody to monitor her condition and take care of her round the clock as her situation could worsen and get out of hand any moment. One could not afford to be complacent or consider leaving her unattended now even for a minute. This was when close family friends and relatives again came forward to help. They took turns in staying and looking after Mayan. As per their convenience and feasibility, they stayed on to attend to her for a week or fortnight respectively.

In spite of having already crossed the 80-year old age bar, Pitaji still maintained his cool and kept his morale high and positive. Yet, the generally kept in check anxiety did surface occasionally in an expression of a sudden spurt of uncontrolled temper and frustration. He would suddenly give vent to his frustration on anyone who was unfortunate to be in the vicinity. Although he would control it quickly, apologise and attempt to make up to the victim for his unreasonable fury. All those around had now become familiar with his behaviour. They had quickly learnt to disregard it and to move on. His thrifty temperament was the other side that one had to deal with also. Nevertheless, in the present situation everyone wisely chose to ignore it. However, barring that, Pitaji's profound faith in his God remained unshaken throughout this trying period of his life.

Now Mayan had become completely bedridden and was dependent even for ensuring her personal hygiene and morning ablution. She was gradually becoming short tempered too. Her constant state of inactivity was resulting in the formation of excessive gas in her tummy, leading to indigestion and a constant state of discomfort. She had been taking some Ayurvedic medication for the same and her system had now become completely addicted to it. Strong oral cancer medication was resulting in ulcers in her stomach and a strong burning sensation as it was not being sufficiently substantiated with a proper food intake. Consequently, her mouth was filled with sores making it hard for her to eat. However much the related doctors tried to reduce the number of medicines, the effort now proved to be a futile exercise as she had to be treated for so many resultant ailments as well. Dr. Vitul could be seen struggling to find a way to reduce their number but they would inevitably sum up to the same count.

A stringent regularity was now being maintained in charting her blood pressure, sugar levels and fever. The doctor was personally on a day-to-day basis monitoring it.

Not just the discomfort but also the pain had started to accentuate. Then her left breast had gradually hardened like stone. The breast skin now glistened like polished stone. The doctors were at sea and completely perplexed as to why that had come to be.

Mayan had slowly begun to retreat within herself. Probably she was now gearing up and preparing herself to face the glaring eventuality staring her in her face. She knew, though she never voiced it that she did not now have long to live. She was now so frail that she could no longer attend her 'satsang'.

So, an arrangement was made where the Satsang recital could be heard in her room itself via a wire connection made to a loudspeaker that was installed in her room.

Mayan had actually had some very enlightening spiritual experiences through the course of her life. Several years ago when her uncle had fallen critically ill, and Mayan in a moment of exhaustion had slipped into deep slumber, she had a vision where her 'Isht' spoke to her. 'He' informed her that he would relieve her uncle of his human existence at 8 a.m. the following morning. The next morning came and she was completely shaken when that is exactly how it happened. It was really nothing next to sheer miracle. So it did not come as a surprise when she now started announcing to her near and dear ones that she would leave them soon after 1st of July.

Vineet had now taken to spending several hours sitting by her side and speaking to her on the essence of life. He spoke of how so far she had always successfully participated in the race of life and now that the clinching moment was fast approaching, there was no way that he would allow her to lose it. "Give up all your other attachments, bonds that constrain your freedom and prevent your perfect amalgamation with the 'Supreme Being', our 'Creator'. Discover this final release and blend with 'Him', lose your identity in 'Him' and the only sound that should now be heard by you is 'His' name, 'His' presence. You are now pitted against 'Death' in this final lap of your life's race. You cannot allow it to outwit you and defeat you now. This is the only and the final meaningful step that one needs to take in one's life. Only when you have rid yourself of those five demons – desires, anger, greed, attachment and ego that you will acquire the pure human form and be able to successfully cross over to amalgamate with your 'Creator'. Do not let this wonderful opportunity that life now offers to you pass by. All your life you have strived for this moment, do not fail now, do not forget that this is the final goal that has led you on so far."

Mayan would then gently nod her head in mild assent. After the paralytic stroke Mayan had mellowed down, her ability to converse distinctly impacted and ever her tonal quality had altered considerably.

To sermonize comes easy but then also ignoring the 'eternal truth' does not make it go away. If one accepts it, all the better, and if one does not, then so be it.

In the meantime as the festival of 'Holi' was coming, riots had broken out in the city of Bareilly. Therefore, Vineet was now called on duty. He requested one of his relatives to fill in for him and to look after Mayan as he was now helpless and couldn't help being away. But probably some pressing issues prevented that gentleman from being able to 'fill in' for Vineet, so he sheepishly expressed his inability to do so. Vineet learnt a lesson that day that everyone has to bear the weight of his own responsibilities, to expect it from any other, however close they be, was improper. He did rue for a moment why he had requested another for the same but then after retrospection and having prayed to the saviour he found some solace.

Adversity is often a capable teacher and the mother of invention. It provides you with an insight into several of those facets of life that man in one's normal circumstances often gives little weightage to and infact often disregards. It unfolds the new horizons, the unread chapters before one and also effectively disintegrates certain impractical, preconceived expectations and notions. Vineet made some alternate arrangements during his absence and soon returned after a gap of 2 days.

After a short gap Suneet returned along with his wife and left her behind to take care of Mayan.

At regular intervals Mayan's suffering would suddenly intensify making her pain insufferable. She would then writhe pitifully with pain and then break down crying in intense agony. Gradually, even the pain injections had stopped being effective. They were no longer able to provide her any relief from her unbearable suffering. So, the doctors were compelled to graduate her to the next step and put her on a low dose of morphine in order to numb her pain. This was actually the last recourse that they could now take. Alternative pain management therapies were also tried out but none provided her with any relief.

Then the doctors even considered putting Mayan on 'radiation therapy' in order to control the spreading cancer nodes but they had to give up this possibility as her blood did not have the sufficient number of platelets that were required to administer it. In fact, the situation had become so precarious that blood donation had to be made on 2-3 occasions to collect the blood and administer it to her in order to bring up her platelet count. But then even this entailed its own share of complications, as when the blood was to be transfused her veins could not be found. The chemoport had already stopped working earlier and had been removed. Tackling this complication became another nightmare.

Pitaji's natural concern and desperation to save Mayan at any cost had convinced him that whatever the complications only 'radiation' would save her. That resulted in some serious altercation, a conflict of opinion and a temporary straining of relationship between Vineet and Pitaji. Pitaji was just not willing to accept the terrible dangers that radiation therapy entailed in Mayan's case. However, Vineet had long accepted it and realized the terrible threat in taking this course of action.

But, very soon as Mayan's condition deteriorated further, Pitaji finally accepted the writing on the wall and he himself gave up insisting on giving her radiation. Mayan's pains had gradually progressed to a point where merely watching her writhe in pain was becoming more and more unbearable. Once, when Vineet had had to go away for a short stint due to his professional obligations she had given vent to her extreme frustration, screaming through the phone's mouthpiece, "Are you waiting to come only after I am gone?" Sensing her trauma and desperation Vineet lost his usually kept in check composure and broke-down. Tears had rolled down his cheeks as he responded to her sobs. Vineet's daughter who had been studying abroad had completed her course. Her convocation was due for which Vineet had applied for leave. Cancelling that, Vineet immediately left to be beside his mother. When he informed his daughter of the same, she herself had endorsed his course of action, "Dad you've done the right thing. Granny needs you more. It is more important that you should be with her. I am also coming over very soon. Convocation can be attended later." That moment Vineet had felt a fresh surge of pride for the values that his daughter had imbibed in her life.

The same granddaughter had so often jokingly chided her granny, "Dadi, don't you ever dare forget that I am the only invaluable granddaughter you have, the rest are all useless grandsons." Then Mayan too would respond in the same light hearted spirit, "But then, you better not forget too that you too have one and only one granny, my darling granddaughter. So don't you forget that either!"

Arranging for the morphine pouches was not proving to be simple, but Vineet managed to get them somehow. Mayan was now put on a regular dose of morphine. Its effect now had resulted in relieving her of her pain to quite some extent. However, under its influence she was no longer alert and seemed to be drugged most of the time. Whenever its effect would wear off a little, Mayan would ask for some devotional hymns to be sung to her. Vineet would very often now sing for her one particular hymn that he knew by rote. That happened to be one of Mayan's favourite ones too, so she would also mumble the words along with him:

'O my Lord, the Immortal!
The saviour of his devotees,
when will you accept me within you?
Beloved Lord! We are Your slaves,
while You are our Bestower!
So direct Your kind glance and shower upon us,
Your benign grace.
Either you enfold us within you,
else we will embrace death,
and-
shed off this human cloak!
The pang of separation is now unbearable,
rid us of this torture,
and grace us with Your enlightened vision!'
(Original verses at page 182)

□

11

Having always believed in following the middle path Mayan had so far tread on life's path moving sensibly and covering the journey of her life with a clear target to reach the final destination. Now she had finally reached very close to what she had strived for all her life. The time was now ripe to reap its true dividends. Once one perceives the goal of one's life's existence then one prepares oneself accordingly and slowly but steadily inches towards that final destination. One can successfully do so only by never detouring from one's path, always keeping in mind that, that and that alone will take one to one's final culmination and eventually find salvation.

Mayan had gradually developed deep insecurities. Lately, she had started holding onto Vineet as her sole source of comfort believing that most of the others around her did not really mean her well. She would constantly cling on to Vineet voicing her concern, "Don't you leave me alone, not even for a second. Whenever you are not around people stop bothering about me, they stop paying any heed to my urgings. Do you know in the intermediate period when you were not here, then this relative who was here to take care of me sent all my attendants on leave and herself too did not bother to attend to me. I was forced to lie in my own excreta for hours. Please help me, take pity and don't reduce me to this state, please."

Vineet was deeply pained on hearing about this harsh reality. However, he refrained from conducting any enquiry or cross checking her complaint. It really would have been a pointless exercise. What was done was done! One couldn't change what had already come to pass. One can't really read on the face accurately, what the other person's true intentions are and the level of their integrity.

Therefore, to be surprised that they would not even spare an already suffering soul would be quite irrational. Probably, it gave such people some sense of depraved satisfaction to do so. After all God has created all kinds that inhabit his world. Actually, they play a very important role, as they become the sources that are instrumental in helping one sever one's ties with this world.

So Vineet advised Mayan, "See every human being in this world comes to play a definite role and to realize a purpose. Probably, God Himself had provided the circumstances to compel her to behave in this callous and indifferent fashion. In fact, you should be grateful to her for actually providing you a reason, thereby making it simpler for you to cut off your ties easily from the rest of this world. And then, above all, you yourself have always motivated us to inculcate the qualities of forbearance, forgiveness and patience, that we should always bear these in our minds when passing through the changing phases of our life, and ...," something had registered with Mayan. Perhaps, now she understood.

Then there were those who happened to have interacted with Mayan, may be a couple of times, yet they had connected with her and had developed a deep bonding with Mayan. So much so that now they devoted their services and time for her with utmost sincerity and commitment. Vineet's close friends and their wives too did more than the needful, taking turns to looking after Mayan. They did their duty as if they were her own flesh and blood. But Mayan too, despite her frail state, was not miserly in her show of affection towards them. Like a doting mother, she fondly ate out of their hands, as if she was being fed by her daughter and in turn badgered them nonstop till they had eaten well too. Though now finding it difficult to speak she still managed to emote and communicate it all through her eyes. Even the attendants had become so attached to Mayan by now that without anybody having to remind them they were on their own accord never leaving Mayan unattended. In fact, during the course of Mayan's sickness, she really was lucky to have with her a couple of attendants who would not hesitate to serve her in any capacity. They willingly performed all levels of duties, whenever and whatever may they be. One of them had actually accompanied Mayan from Lucknow on her own accord to look after her in Agra. They had all gradually grown so close to Mayan and now were treated as an integral part of her family itself.

Still, no one could now ignore the stark reality that was becoming more and more evident that Mayan had very limited time left. The clock was ticking away, fast bringing the dreaded day closer and closer. Both Vineet and Anjali had now come to stay and look after Mayan for an extended period. Suneet too was frequently coming from Delhi to spend time with Mayan. Mayan's youngest son, who had long ago settled abroad, had been informed as well. He immediately made his plan to fly down and be with her.

The word had spread that it was a matter of a few days only that Mayan would no more be with them. The doctors too had indirectly given the indication to the same effect. Many acquaintances, relatives now started visiting her to seek her last blessings. Some came to fulfil a formality. "Baiji will soon be leaving us. We thought it was only proper to come and visit her," was their worldly reasoning. One such concerned gentleman, very sincerely following the customary code of social conduct actually put a 500 rupee currency note in her hand, little realizing that the person in whose hand he had placed the amount was unaware of even her own presence leave alone that 500 rupee note. What a mindless exercise it was to try to draw such a person into the so-called perfunctory motions! One who had now reached the last stage of her earthly existence and was actually dangling by a weak thread that was keeping her hanging between life and death. She was now grimly fighting to gain victory over death. But why be judgmental, after all every person has his own level of understanding and perception about life. It is also commonly said, "a particular person will behave in a particular fashion because he can behave in no other." He cannot change until and unless his inner voice beckons him to do so but then such instances are really very rare and far between.

Mayan was now running on borrowed time. It was now necessary for her to undergo a complete radical change in her mental and emotional perception of life. To first stop the morphine injection in order to draw her out from under its drugging influence and then to ensure an alert receptivity from Mayan where she focuses her entire concentration and dedicates it to amalgamating with the 'Father' above, to the complete exclusion of all else was no mean task. Vineet realized that he was now faced with another foreboding task. He would repeatedly remind her of her past experiences and interaction with the holy saints of her cult. He spoke of the times when she had been fortunate to serve them the few times they had accepted her hospitality and visited her at her home. Whenever he spoke of those moments, Mayan would suddenly come out of her trance and be galvanized for some time but then very soon she would slip back into a depression again. Vineet would then narrate some holy tales that he had grown up hearing and would make a desperate yet a studied attempt to recharge her again. Two such tales that he often narrated to her in an attempt to drive home his point were as follows - the first one began thus - "Once there lived a very rich man who set out on a journey in search of God. He happened to meet a thug on the way who finding in the rich man a possible victim suggested - 'look if you really want to discover God I can lead you to him. Trusting the thug the rich man followed him. The thug then led the unsuspecting man to a well and advised him, 'If you should enter into this well you shall then meet God.' The foolish man believing the thug handed over all his belongings to the thug and jumped into the well. The thug having achieved his goal immediately took off with the rich man's belongings. In the meanwhile the rich man, as he fell into the well, happened to strike his forehead against a huge stone that was lying in the water. But, lo and behold! What do you think followed. God actually appeared before him! And then what followed was another miracle. Thanks to the mercy of God a passerby heard his call for help and helped him to come out of the well unscathed. He happily returned home. It was just a coincidence that only a few days later the thug and the rich man's paths crossed again.

On noticing the thug, the rich man started to move towards him. Realizing that he was cornered, the thug started to run. The rich man followed suit for quite some distance until he finally caught up with the thug. The thug then fell down at his feet begging for mercy. But much to the thug's surprise the rich man in turn caught hold of the thug's feet and pleaded, "Oh no, not at all, you are not a thief. In fact, you are my 'Guru', you are the one who lead me to God, you guided me, showing me the path that took me to my Lord. Whatever else happened is immaterial to me."

Mayan who had been listening to the tale with total and rapt attention, now commented, "Yes, and do you know this tale is also there in the discourse of our Gurus."

"So then ma, now when you are being lead on the path that will lead you to your Creator, you should too in fact express your profuse gratitude and thanks to all those who are helping you to reach 'Him'. Bear no grudge, no animosity towards anyone. In fact, humbly ask for forgiveness from all, in case you have hurt somebody's feelings and emotions untowardly or unknowingly. Even if so far you have borne some ill, some pent up anger against anyone, let it go off and forgive the concerned soul. They have all actually played a major role in your upliftment and helped you to evolve as a pure soul. They, whom you feel have done you the most injustice, are actually the source that has cleansed you the most. They, who have been your worst critics, have treated you shabbily and scorned you the most, deserve to be hailed the maximum by you for helping you to inch closer to this glorious moment of salvation," Vineet murmured into Mayan's ear. Mayan then slowly opened her eyelids, her lips shook and an expression of pure tender love flitted across her facial features.

Vineet playfully fondled her hair and reprimanded her, while tapping her gently on her forehead, "Yes Ma that includes me too. You need to detach yourself from me as well. I should be no exception to the rule either. Get to the essence of your purpose in life now. Try to understand what I am trying to communicate to you. I do not need to explain to you that you now need to move under the expansive shadow of your Creator. Once you move under 'His' shade, then you will be safe forever."

Mayan reacted, blinked her eyes and then shook her head befuddled. A question mark was writ clearly across her face as if to say, "Just what are you saying?"

"Oh Ma, have you forgotten what grandma so often said? Have you actually forgotten the tale that we heard from her innumerable times – Once a merchant lying on his deathbed beckoned his son to approach him and then advised his son to take good care of their shop and business ensuring that it grew and prospered. He further went on to give him a warning too, that in this effort, however, he should also ensure that he only walks under a shaded path to reach his destination. The foolish son, wrongly imbibing his father's parting advice invested all his money in creating a canopy that provided shade leading right from his shop to his home. A well-wisher finally explained to the fool, "Your father had only meant that you should put in your sincere effort and only then will you succeed, that is, start your day early, rise before sunrise and get to work early in the wee hours of the morning, work hard the whole day and return home only after sunset. Then will you taste success," so saying Vineet completed the story.

A hint of a smile now crossed Mayan's face and she whispered in a barely audible voice, "What a complete fool he was!"

"So this is exactly what I have been trying to tell you. You cannot afford to commit a similar stupidity. So dear ma, keep your eyes now fixed on your final goal, the purpose, and the essence of your life. Do not let your attention waiver. Have you forgotten what the great sage Kabir has said:

"Close your eyes, your ears and
your lips to this world;
internalize to hear and then absolve,
the eternal sound-
that reverberates
in the higher spiritual climes!"
(Original verses at page 182)

From this moment on, I will not allow anybody to encroach on your time and attention. Concentrate on the Creator, your Benefactor alone. I will provide you with his soothing remembrances via hymns that have been sung in his praise," Vineet mind was now made.

Mayan seemed to draw some energy after Vineet was done with his discourse, so she gently nodded her head in approval.

Vineet continued to sing a few couplets from Kabir's writings:

"Our future remains unpredictable!
However, we can ensure that our deeds are noble,
our intentions honourable,
and we forget 'Him' not, reinforced
with repeated utterances of his Holy name!
Man spends his energy,
accruing wealth that is wrongly amassed
through deceitful and illegal practices.
He cannot be trusted,
as his speech is fraudulent and untrue.
Thus, man is actually not amassing wealth-
but in fact, weighing himself down,
with a load of sinful actions,
so much so that there can then be no possibility-
of ridding himself of this unholy load!
The mind is like the elephant that has lost control,
the body is only a pile of this earth,
one's span of life is eeking out,
with every passing minute,
hence you have no recourse.
The only hope now lies in chanting-
His holy name,
with every breath of your remaining life!"
As long as the "SOUL" resides in your physical form,
you may bask and enthral in the base desires;
but what when it departs,
reducing you to mere dust?

So prepare to shed the lust, the greed, the anger-
and your runaway ego,
and instead fill your inherent self with kindness and care.
Strive for a sense of detachment-
from this so transitory a world,
and soak in the wisdom of life!"
(Original verses at page 182)

Pitaji also tried his best in all possible ways to enhance Mayan's spiritual inclination. He often recited the following couplets from the Holy verse:

"Departing from the bodily form,
to find refuge in the spiritual,
the soul is thus elevated
to its intrinsic purer form!"
(Original verses at page 183)

He often repeated to Mayan, "Through the worldly sufferings, God mitigates the *karmik* burden. This is the disguised way of 'His' divine blessings that expedite the process of salvation." Mayan would then whisper, 'I too realize it. I humbly pray to God that he may put me through whatever sufferings I have to undergo, but 'He' should simultaneously grant me the strength to bear it.' Pitaji further reminded Mayan of the great assurance God had given to His disciples:

"I am concerned about your well-being,
will take due care of all your worries;
so what is the need for you to fret-
shed all uncertainties,
just nurture love for Me!"
(Original verses at page 183)

Mayan was now slowly internalising and finding solace as well as the energy from within her to rise above her worldly sufferings. She had almost stopped making any verbal communication with those around her. Her food intake had now gone down to almost the bare minimum, probably her gullet had narrowed down with the rapidly growing cancer that was fast gaining ground. On one hand, the cancer nodes had ripened to reach the terminating stage and on the other her emotional and mental bonds were setting themselves free. Her face now carried an uncomplicated serene expression almost like that of an unsuspecting little child that is unafraid and oblivious to life's threats and challenges. Having so far pursued the middle path Mayan had already come a long way covering the major course of her life. So now she needed to reach the finishing point, the ultimate goal successfully. At this juncture in life what remains would be the fruit of how one reaches this stage in one's life, one's actions through the course of one's life whether noble or otherwise, that would now determine the final outcome. One who undertakes this arduous journey of worldly existence and follows the right path, ensuring a purity of deed and purpose throughout, is better equipped to cross this final hurdle and attain salvation.

If through life's journey one has wavered from one's course and has not followed the path that would eventually lead one to the final Gateway that could open, then one will lose the right track and will never be able to reach the 'Gate', let alone wait for it to open. Has one drawn from one's worldly existence the positive energy, the sustenance and the infinite force to cross over? This issue requires serious introspection! Whenever a family is faced with such a circumstance, it should be accepted and solicited as an auspicious moment. All should unite and partake in that solemn occasion. These provide an opportunity to those around to dwell in self-introspection too. Unfortunate are those that do not find time or are unable to share these glorious last moments with their earthly parents who are actually the medium that will provide them finally with this glorious opportunity to enter that beautiful world where one amalgamates with the 'Benefactor'! They lose forever that invaluable chance to seek their parents' last blessings and to realize the real value of being in this world.

The ultimate purpose of life is to avail of the awareness and the ability to contemplate the real purpose of one's existence rather than mere worldly survival.

□

12

It is not easy for the simple human mind to realize that to relinquish this world is in fact the doorway that leads one to one's spiritual birth. To realize that the death of one's human form is an exalted leap that lends significant and incomparable meaning to one's life takes time and effort. Otherwise, everything else in life actually holds little or no meaning at all.

Then, the 1st of July finally arrived. Mayan had been anxiously awaiting its arrival, as it was the birth anniversary of her 'Guru'. She celebrated the day with complete devotion. She insisted on visiting 'His sacred seat' and paying her homage to 'Him' in person. Therefore, her family respecting her wish took her on a wheel chair to fulfil her wish. Probably, this was her way of convincing herself that her 'Creator' now wanted that her last wish should be that "God now should take her under 'His' benign care forever. She was ready to come to 'Him' to take refuge under 'His' holy presence."

Surprisingly, Mayan had already repeatedly declared that, "I will leave you all after the 1st of July." Others, probably had paid little heed to her declaration, but it had registered and left its impact in the minds of both Pitaji and her son, Vineet. Both of them often pondered on her words wondering what was to come next.

Vineet in the mean time persisted in his effort. It was his innate wish and conviction that he needed to try his level best to help Mayan enhance her level and attain spiritual upliftment. He would keep whispering into her ears now and then, "'Force' has two forms - one in the form of 'light' and the other is in the form of 'sound' – let the name of God resound internally within and fill up your entire self with the holy current. Draw unto yourself your Guru's spiritual form and attach yourself with his infinite self forever. Let your soul resume its sublime form – 'Radha'. Give up forever all worldly attachments and attractions that pull you down. Only then can you prepare to amalgamate and become one with the Almighty the 'Soami'. 'Radhasoami' is thus the state of being 'one' with the Supreme Being who is the ultimate. This is the sole purpose of the human form and the only route to attain 'salvation'. Purify yourself so that nothing prevents you from experiencing the brilliance of the 'Eternal'. That would then completely enfold you, surround you and engulf you in its holy aura. Therefore, go on persisting now in your effort and reach that stage where 'Radha' loses its identity to her 'Soami' to attain 'Parmarth', the ultimate meaning, the eventual self."

Mayan would hear him with rapt attention and then make the effort to follow it. Vineet's purpose now was to help her release all her attachments to this world and become a detached soul ready to enter the 'other'. The most meaningful service that you can render to a soul standing at the threshold of his earthly departure is to help one take the leap and free one from all other bondages. Vineet would remind Mayan often that, "The Guru himself has sermonised that holding on to one's worldly possessions and attachments and yet hoping to connect with the Creator is impossible. One needs to realize first that the two worlds are intrinsically different, and in essence, there exists no congruence between the two. So when you seek anything from 'God', it should be nothing but 'Him' and 'Him' alone. To pray to 'Him' for anything other than 'Him', would be to demean the Lord's dignity and benevolence."

Vineet would also often take refuge in the examples given in the holy scriptures of other sects and religious beliefs –

"The world saw Lord Jesus being crucified which thereby implies that even 'God' only after 'He' had severed all worldly connections and risen to 'His' sublime and pure form was then paid obeisance to, as the 'Son' of 'God'. Therefore, you now need to accept it, ma, that the cancer that has conquered your human form is actually that 'crucifying cross' that will help you relinquish forever this worldly connection. So do not let go off this chance offered by the ordinance of God. Then, how can you forget that when God had appeared before Hajrat Abrahim he had had this revelation that if there was anything or anyone that was an intrusion and was coming between his implicit love for God, the Creator, then he needed to remove that obstacle. It was then that Hajrat realizing that his own son, his own flesh and blood stood between God and him, had found the courage to sacrifice his own son in deference with the wishes of 'Khuda', in order to surrender himself totally to 'Him'. Then, God appreciating the extent of Hajratji's commitment to 'Him', Hajratji was awarded with a pristine white lamb as a symbol of innocence and purity. So now let the realization dawn upon yourself too and disassociate yourself completely destroying all your earthly bindings that are preventing you from becoming one with the Creator."

This is what 'Shiva's Tandav' also denotes that is – churn out from within you all those worldly connections, destroy and then detach yourself totally from this earthly existence of yours. Then, and only then, will you be successful in opening Shiva's third eye and become one with the 'Lord'. 'He' alone is now your father, your husband and your son.

Burn to cinders this delusion that this earthly home is your permanent abode. Sant Kabir has so appropriately philosophised this reality. He says, "Do not lose your path and fade away into the oblivion. There is only one Name that will live on forever and that is 'God's' holy presence." Vineet chiding her affectionately persisted, "Evolve, as God's true devotee with a devotion as complete as 'Meera' who revered Lord Krishna and was oblivious to all else. Love and devote yourself to God with the same level of intensity. Do not forget that you too belong to the same land that Meera Bai hailed from. Are you paying heed to what I am saying?"

A doctor friend of Vineet had once commented lightly, "Why are you killing your own mother with this ridiculous logic of yours? After all she is the one who brought you into this world!" There must have been some logic, some reasoning behind this statement of the doctor. However, if he were to see it through Vineet's eyes then the departure of Mayan from this world held a completely new meaning, a different level of logical reasoning and acceptance for Vineet. He had perceived a meaningful purpose behind man's life journey on its onset with the 'art of living' and its culmination with the mastering of the 'art of dying'. Vineet only wanted to ensure that his mother Mayan succeeded in this life's ethereal mission. Now the 'death' of her human form would lead her to a doorway that would result in her new spiritual birth. Man takes time to register finally that 'Death' in this world is actually an exalted step, the forward leap that finally takes you to realize your true purpose of this earthly existence. All else is irrelevant and transitory.

For the following couple of days Mayan continued with this process of internalisation. Then on the 5th of July, Mayan's birthday finally arrived. Her family members celebrated it in a sombre yet meaningful manner. There was a method in that day's activity, a 'Satsang' where close associates congregated to recite the holy verses and remember the God above, eulogizing his magnanimity and generosity towards his subjects whether it be the good or the erring. Then 'Prasad', God's blessings in the form of sweets were distributed to all only after it had first been offered at the Lord's feet. That was followed by her birthday celebrations. Innumerable photographs were taken. Mayan in a quiet composed demeanour did whatever was asked of her. Then, offerings were first placed in Mayan's hands, symbolic of her making these offerings and were then placed at the feet of the 'guru' in the 'Gurudwara'. She then made some charitable contribution for the lesser fortunate, the needy and the poor.

Vineet's leave was now finally ending. He needed to go to Lucknow to join office at least for a day and then apply afresh for further leave to return to Agra. Therefore, after the birthday celebrations he left for Lucknow late that very evening and arrived at Lucknow station after 10 p.m. He had just descended, his feet having barely touched the Lucknow railway platform when he received a frantic call from Anjali. "The doctor had come to check Mayan's condition. He says that the 'time' has come, Mayan can leave us anytime now."

Vineet immediately rushed to his Chief's house, reaching around 11.30 p.m. at night. He briefed him about the urgency of the situation, as now it was a 'touch and go' situation for his mother. The Chief immediately responded, "Do not waste a single minute waiting for the morning to arrive. Leave immediately. You know I could not be by my mother's bedside when she undertook her 'final journey' for her 'heavenly abode' and I still rue the fact that I could not be there when she left us forever. So don't waste time, leave."

Thanking God for ensuring this support and understanding from his senior Vineet left for Agra. Early the next morning on the 6th of July, he was by her bedside.

Mayan slowly opened her eyes and communicated all that she had yearned all along to tell him, her son, Vineet. Sometimes words can belie silent communication. What one communicates through the silence then needs no words to express ones sentiments. Vineet continued to utter some gentle proddings into her ear, "One needs to make oneself ready for the final journey and then undertake it alone. This world is a temporary stop over where you camp, take shelter for a short while, and then proceed towards the final destination. Now, you have to move on to reach your real home, your final shelter. Proceed on the rest of your journey positively with contentment and pride. The path that takes you to meet your Lord finally may be uphill, arduous and a little trying but the final fruit is going to be worth its while. So go on, cross over and never look back."

The doctor arrived in the afternoon. Mayan was finding it increasingly difficult to swallow food. So it was concurred that a tube needed to be put to transfer liquid nourishment into her system. Vineet was a little sceptical. However, the consensus was that the tube should be arranged, as there seemed no real harm in giving it a trial. Though, still apprehensive, Vineet gave his consent. As arranging for the tube was taking sometime, Dr. Vitul left with the suggestion that, "Dr. Satsangi is an experienced doctor and lives right here in the neighbourhood itself. He can be called to put it once the tube has been brought." Dr. Satsangi was then contacted on phone. He immediately responded and agreed to do the needful. Even otherwise, being a next-door neighbour he had always maintained good and healthy relations with them. In fact over the years, he had developed a deep affinity and attachment with the family. Often the family to treat some little niggling health issues that surfaced suddenly at some odd hour would consult him.

Just then, Mayan beckoned her personal attendant to approach her and whispered, "Look, you have served me sincerely. It is now time for me to leave you all. But I will be at peace wherever I am only if I can be sure that Pitaji will be well attended to and properly looked after. Promise me that you will serve Pitaji as you have served me all this while." Then, mustering together whatever little energy she still had left in her she beckoned Pitaji to come near her. Responding immediately Pitaji came by her side and bending down whispered in her ear, "Don't worry I am right here beside you." Mayan slowly opened her eyes and looked deep into his eyes as if she was taking one hard final look to assimilate and then successfully stow away his image within her. Closing her eyes tight, she once again retreated into her world within.

□

13

In the purest of its form her 'soul' was now being pulled towards 'Divinity', to find its original abode which is 'its' final resting place. Actually, in a way she was now reliving her entire life in that single spur of that divine moment. The Hindu mythology dictates that a single breath of 'Brahma', the Creator, carries innumerable eras. It is difficult for a mere man to visualize this as there is a yawning distance between man's perception of the 'time cycle' and the actual 'wheel of time', God's creation.

Dr. Satsangi had arrived. The tube that was meant to feed Mayan had to be fitted now. It was probably predestined that Mayan's core family should all be present then. In fact, Anjali's husband, Mayan's son-in-law was also by her side then. He had come to see her and was preparing to leave after lunch. But, when the doctor arrived he stayed on to watch the developments. Mayan's youngest son who had settled abroad also happened to have arrived only a few days back. The presence of all the core family members was indeed a fortunate coincidence. Mayan was securely cocooned all around by all her near and dear ones at this, one of the two most vital moments of a human being's life. One being when he enters this world and takes on the earthly existence and the second when he prepares to leave it in order to return to his real abode, under the secure canopy of his 'Creator'. Vineet was standing by her side gently pressing her hand to reassure her. The doctor made two attempts to pass the tube through her nose, but the effort proved to be unsuccessful, as every time the tube would slip out. Pitaji stood anxiously behind the doctor watching over the proceedings, while Anjali stood by Mayan's feet gently caressing her at short intervals as if trying to give her assurance that all would be well. The rest of the family was moving in and out of the room as the situation demanded. Just then, Mayan opened her eyes for a flash of a second to direct her glance straight at Vineet. It was indeed Vineet's good fortune that he was at that moment tenderly gazing at her face while affectionately moving his fingers through her hair to provide her any possible comfort, any little reassurance that would help in mitigating some of the pain that she was probably experiencing during the doctor's repeated clinical manoeuvres to insert the tube. Their eyes then met and interlocked for a fraction of a second. Then closing her eyes while heaving a deep sigh of acceptance Mayan breathed her last. Vineet experienced a sharp wave that flashed through his entire body like a current suddenly engulfing him. The doctor immediately responded in an effort to revive her. But Vineet already knew that it was a futile exercise as they had lost Mayan forever; she had left them now never to return. The doctor knew it too but then as per the medical professional norms, he went through the entire process of carefully checking her heart's palpitation and respiration before declaring, "Please pour the holy water in her mouth" and then turning to Pitaji pronounced, "Dear brother, she has left us for her heavenly abode."

Pitaji stood transfixed, rooted to his spot, as tears slowly rolled down his cheeks. Realizing that Pitaji may any minute now lose his composure and sink into depression, Vineet immediately reached by his side holding his hand, "Father, we need to immediately go to the *Satsang* place, the residence of *Guruji* and bowdown before the Supreme Being for His mercy and offer our humble obeisance at his feet for taking Mayan into his Divine care. This is the most pious moment where Mayan's soul has now melted into its Divine form. This is that divine hour that Mayan had prayed for all her life. Today her wish has been finally fulfilled. It is a blessed moment indeed, for all of us, "So let us remember and thank God for his benign mercy."

Pitaji gradually composing himself began to chant in a soft undertone "You my Lord are our Benefactor, our guide and mentor. Provide us the guidance and the strength to accept your decision." He then proceeded to put on his shoes and went towards *Kothi* (house of *Guru*, the *Satsang* place) as fast as his frail feet could carry him. A concerned Vineet asked a relative standing nearby to accompany Pitaji in case he should miss a step and fall. As per one's level of individual understanding, many relatives and acquaintances responded accordingly. Some went into deep mourning, some just stood there maintaining a quiet composure without any apparent reaction, while some bowed their heads before the Deity to pray for the departed soul's peace, final release and comfort. After having paid homage to the Almighty, Pitaji had barely turned to retrace his steps when the *Satsang* hall reverberated with renditions of the prayers. The first verse went as follows:

Departing from the bodily form,
to find refuge in the spiritual,
the soul has elevated to its intrinsic purer form!
(Original verses at page 183)

These were the very pious words that Pitaji had often recited to console Mayan in her last days.

Whether this was mere chance or God's ordinance is beyond human understanding. Mayan who had entered this world on the 5th of July left it on the 6th of July. Her prophecy that she would leave this world in the beginning of the month had come true. The culmination of her worldly life followed just after the centenary celebration of her spiritual mentor. And the day Lord chose to take her in His gracious lap was the day after her birthday, after she had fulfilled her wish to do charity, to participate in a 'Satsang' session, to feed the poor and to distribute sweets amongst all. A satisfied and purified soul she had quietly bid adieu to this world and her people. She, in her purest form of 'Radha', had been drawn towards her 'Creator', the *'Soami'* for abode at the absolute divine region. Looking at its deeper meaning she had left fulfilled after having lived out her entire life on earth in that fractional divine moment when her soul finally quit its earthly form to blend with the 'Infinite'. As the Hindu belief and saying goes, 'Brahma, the originator engulfs within each single breath innumerable centuries'. Human perception of the passing of time is poles apart from the real 'wheel of time'. Kabir, the great saint had philosophised, "This is the world of the dead...". Another rejoinder made by the saintly, the honest 'Dharmaraj Yudhishthir of the epic 'Mahabharata' fame, when asked was, "What is man's biggest folly?" and Yudhishthir had replied, - "Man observes others die and leave this world around him each day yet nurtures the fallacy that he himself will live on forever." He, who has taken birth in this world, has to die and leave it behind. Moreover, this is applicable to even God himself after 'He' chooses to incarnate in the human form and takes birth to come into this world. So then if God Himself is not spared the cycle how can a mere man expect it to be otherwise?

Introspection would then reveal that even when the world was a 'naught' there was the 'ONE' still present embodying within 'Itself' the centre of all energy. Then this energy divulged itself, the 'Centrifugal force' divided itself into several layer after layer of that 'latent' force, that energy.

This diversified energy that was born through 'naught' then created its miniscule form of energy which then gradually multiplied again to generate the diverse forms of matter that are present on earth. And those generations of evolving forms eventually resulted in the birth of the human form which is considered to be the most superior and the most evolved of all the living beings present in their life form. To elevate to a higher form, one has to revert to the human form. Therefore, it is inevitable to 'enter into' and then 'to exit' the human form. In fact out of the two, the process of 'exit' is spiritually more critical and of greater import.

Mayan had finally realized the purpose of her existence in this world after she had experienced all its difficulties and had finally acquired its pristine mould and form. Mayan had always held her mother-in-law in very high esteem and had sincerely incorporated several of her teachings into her own life's value systems. However, the only person whom Mayan had actually deified was her mother-in-law's younger brother, a truly evolved soul, a true saint who had been Mayan's ultimate guide, directing her actions throughout her life. To rationalize this conviction of hers is meaningless as it is a matter of one's personal ideology and belief. Any attempt to dissect it would further require one to be evolved enough. To actually reach those heights and have the audacity to dare and delve in it requires no mean effort.

Further, Mayan had also fulfilled the promise she had made to her mother that "now as she had become an integral part of her husband's family, she would always pursue the path that would lead to the betterment of her husband and his family and that her loyalties would always remain with them right unto her death." She was indeed fortunate that she had left for her heavenly abode in the presence of her husband. She had remained married to her earthly husband here and then been accepted by her Lord above in her divine form too. The parting expression on her face was a reflection of absolute serenity and divine grace. Pain, suffering, sadness were nowhere to be perceived in that divine glow that now lit her face.

On Pitaji's return after making his offerings to the Lord, Vineet had another proposition to make. He suggested, "it is an auspicious day; let us organise 'Prasad' during the day's last prayer at the 'Bhajan Ghar' (meditation camp) and have it distributed to all the devotees. Let us also feed the poor and do other possible charities. This is the apt hour for humble worship, offerings and contemplation to remember 'Him' who is our originator and thank him." Pitaji himself a strong conformist of his Faith needed no further goading. He was completely of the same view as well and immediately went about arranging for the same.

As is customary, once after the word had gone around about Mayan's demise people began to filter in to offer their condolence and mourn her leaving. However, contrary to their expectation the scenario that presented itself before them was altogether unexpected. The conventional believers reacted strongly and raised their objections insisting that the usual rituals and norms needed to be followed, as it was perfunctorily required at such an hour. The spiritual significance of such events failed to convince their worldly logic and they reacted sharply.

"This is indeed strange. We had come to offer our solemn condolence and look at them here. If they do not seem to want it, then so be it" and left. Pitaji's parting request was "Please do join us in the holy discourse." Unmindful of their reactions Vineet had several other thoughts racing though his mind - Mayan would get up early and pray to the 'Divine' and when turning in for the night she would again kneel down and pray. Vineet realized that her entire life had been a process of remembering the Lord seeking his forgiveness during the course of each day. She had lived her entire life that way. Therefore, Vineet was of the firm conviction that all else was irrelevant and of little consequence. Now that she had left, they needed to pay their final homage to her by devoting the maximum time praying, contemplating and with all humility pleading for the Lord's forgiveness. To reflect and to divulge one's energy in any other farcical and socially expected norms and rites was immaterial and unnecessary. This was the moment when they needed to allow the mind not to defer or drift.

The last rites of Mayan were performed and her body offered to the pious flames. All the members of the family had congregated to perform these last farewell rites. The immediate family members in the house continued to deliver the holy renditions for several days. Whosoever wanted to partake of these holy moments was welcome to join.

Finally, all the family and friends got together and a 'Bhandara', that is, the holy feast was organized. Thousands came and extended their blessings to the family. Mayan's era had ended. It was curtains for her.

□

14

Mayan would often say, "There are some people who are God sent to us. They are neither our blood kin nor wedded into our family yet they manage to find a place close to our heart and become more dear to us than our own."

Vineet and Pitaji were now trying to deliberate how they needed to proceed henceforth. Pitaji now would need to condition himself to staying alone, all by himself. The first few months were bound to be difficult till he, both mentally and emotionally, resigned himself to finally accept the reality that now he had to manage it all by himself. Vineet offered solutions as per his rationale, "There is one and only one rule of the thumb to remain happy in this world and that, is to keep yourself fruitfully involved and busy both physically and mentally. One needs to face life with a pro-active and positive approach to it." But then Pitaji was already completely engrossed in the 'Satsang', therefore, he really didn't have to look any further for more ways of keeping himself busy. His daily routine already involved his attending the Satsang multiple times during the course of the day which was followed by frequent interactions with the other satsangis, where long discourses, discussions were conducted deliberating on different aspects of the day's discourse. So Pitaji was amply involved and already keeping himself sufficiently busy during the day. He did not really need to bother about how he would utilise his time.

Vineet then came up with a new suggestion, "I think it would be a noble deed if we were to go and hold a special 'Satsang and Bhog' in the village that Mayan hails from, her original home before she was wedded to you, Pitaji. We would hence have paid off any remaining dues that we may still be carrying on our shoulders."

Pitaji most happily agreed with Vineet's sentiments. So a day and date was decided upon and preparations began accordingly. To put matters in a clear perspective there was no denying that after the passing away of Mayan's parents the following generation had completely ignored Mayan's presence. They had shown little concern or care for her welfare. However, one of Vineet's maternal grandfather's very dear friend, who was addressed as 'Vaidyaraj' in Mayan's village had always cared very deeply for Mayan. He was genuinely attached to her and had treated her like his own daughter. Whenever Mayan would visit her village, he would take due care of her ensuring that she did not feel the loss of her parents during her stay there.

Almost as if she could forecast what the future would hold for Mayan, her mother had often told Vaidyaraji that after she left this world she expected him to take Mayan under his care and custody. And that is how things eventually turned out to be. Vaidyaraji over the years had gradually come to become genuinely fond of Mayan and had begun to treat her as his very own daughter. In fact, even his son had begun to treat her as his sister. He had become so attached to Mayan and Pitaji that he too considered them to be his own near and dear relatives. Vaidyaraji and his family had thus filled the vacuum that Mayan had in her life.

A similar happy coincidence had come to pass in her husband's family. Mayan's grand mother-in-law too had no real brother. She would often complain to her mother and accuse her of depriving her of the joy of having a brother to give her the security that only a brother can give. She would often pray to God asking Him to give her one. And then it so happened that one of the relatives of the family-priest happened to come in very close contact with them. Gradually, such a deep bond had developed between him and Mayan's grand mother-in-law that he gradually took over the role of her elder brother, fulfilling all the responsibilities that came along with it.

Blessed are those who are bestowed with such meaningful relationships, a bond that proves to be stronger and more lasting than with a blood kin.

Her original home, her abode where Mayan had spent her entire childhood before she had left for her husband's home, those little niches, those windows and those doorways that still remained stowed away in her memory bank, all of which were still connected with her cherished childhood moments but were now locked away under a lock and key and no longer accessible to her.

Both the whereabouts of those who had locked up the house and the destination for which they had left remained a mystery. In fact only a few days before the terrible sickness that had overtaken Mayan, she had visited the village to attend a marriage. She had then come nurturing the longing to relive her childhood days by spending a couple of nights in her home. Alas! Little did she know then that this wish would remain unfulfilled forever. She had hung around in the surrounding premises wistfully watching that huge lock at the entrance of her home that clearly sent a definite warning message that the house no longer welcomed her. She had stood there, a mute spectator and then quietly left along with Vineet who had accompanied her on that trip to her village. He had in those moments experienced and shared her pain but then they were helpless. It was at that juncture that Mayan had finally given up all hope of ever visiting the house again. She had made peace with the fact that 'Vaidyarajji's household was now her sole connection with the village. The sequences of events after that had finally culminated with her last rites that were being performed from her new home in the village. A blissful, peaceful environment had prevailed throughout the 'Satsang' that had been conducted at Vaidyarajji's house. A touching rendition by 'Meera', the devotee of Lord Krishna who had bequeathed her entire life to the Lord's service was also sung in the Satsang. It went as follows:

O you! The protector of the poor and the humble,
I stand here imploring to please you,
open your eyelids and sanctify me with Your Holy glance.
Hear I stand in quest of you and your kind look;
waiting in absolute submission,
ready to give my wretched self in Your final care!
To You who are the very semblance of kindness and forgiveness;
You even endowed salvation on "AHILYA",
who had been reduced to stone,
and lay in the depths of deep dense forest-
for years unattended and uncared!
Yet here I stand deprived,
awaiting your kind mercy,
whereas I weigh only a fraction!!
(Original verses at page 183)

That day the entire village community had been invited to a solemn feast organized in the memory of Mayan. It was truly nothing short of a miracle that as the number of the villagers participating in the feast kept on burgeoning, so did the quantity of food required to be served to them. It was as if Mayan was showering her last blessings on the villagers so as if to fulfil her last obligations towards the land where she had been born and reared.

In his mother's village, Vineet was still remembered fondly for his childhood pranks. Bemused the villagers declared, "Guess what, this is that same mischief monger who had leapt off the first floor of his window." Vineet of course had no memory of that incident. However, he had heard his mother often narrate to her friends and acquaintances the entire sequence of that event. She would often endearingly speak of those innumerable heartaches that she had had to undergo during his childhood days, thanks to his unending unpredictable pranks. When he had jumped off the window from the first floor, Mayan happened to be present there and saw him fall. So she had screamed frantically, "Mother, Vineet is falling, please hold him." Fortunately, Vineet's grandma happened to be bending just below the window in order to pick something from the floor.

A little perplexed she had looked up and involuntarily stretched her arms and Vineet had fallen into them. However, the impact of the fall was such that she could not hold on to him. He had slipped from her arms and fallen, hitting his head hard against the jutting edge of a stone slab that happened to be lying there. It was sheer good fortune that he had first landed into her arms as that had resulted in minimizing the magnitude of the impact of the fall. Otherwise, it could have resulted in very grave injury that could have had serious consequences.

This very grandma of Vineet had been universally popular amongst all and sundry in the village, thanks to her extremely generous and helpful temperament. Perhaps, Mayan had inherited the same qualities from her. Vineet's grandma too was a very religious lady whose belief in her 'deity' was firm and unshakable. Mayan happened to be her only child. This, was a time when social prejudices were deep-rooted and people had extremely marred social perceptions where delivering a 'boy' was like achieving victory over a 'herculean task' thereby making you eligible to special treatment and adornment. However, if found wanting, you would find yourself at the receiving end of constant reprimands and humiliating barbs. These were flung at you constantly thereby making your existence extremely miserable. This prejudice was one of the black marks of the old orthodox Indian society. Mayan had watched her mother suffer these constant humiliations, as she had not given birth to a son. But, when Mayan became the mother of three bonny sons, grandma's world underwent a complete change. She would now go about the village preening and expansively declaring with immense pride, "My daughter is the mother of three sons. So what if I had no sons, she has more than made up for it. This is the 'justice of Fate'. None present here now dare point a finger at me." Mayan too would gloat with the perceived satisfaction that her mother could now bask in the reflected glory of her three grandsons. That she was responsible for helping her mother rid herself of that stigma gave her a feeling of immense happiness too. Mayan would often talk about related past experiences in this context. And today, Mayan's sons accompanied by their father had come to pay their respect and express their gratitude to all those villagers who had congregated for the peace of the departed soul and had extended their goodwill and blessing.

After Pitaji had completed all the necessary social rites that were needed to ensure the complete release and emancipation of the departed noble soul, he then applied himself to taking up the task of the distribution of Mayan's belongings to those who had sincerely served her and had held her in high esteem and regard. Pitaji, with a complete openness of heart and generosity gave away all her well-preserved clothes, jewellery and those valuable assets that she had collected over the years. However at the same time, he kept back a few of those appropriate belongings that would be passed onto her future generations. Some accepted them as a source of her reminiscence, while others took them for their worldly value. While this activity was proceeding, Vineet's mind had wandered back. He remembered Mayan's words, "Some people are sent to us by God Himself as 'His' messengers to unwittingly associate with us and gradually become a more integral part of us than our own blood kin. They touch our hearts leaving a permanent impression that then lasts throughout a lifetime! They come to be held so close to our heart that they become our very own." Vineet was now reminded of all those who had so intimately touched their lives at sometime or the other during the course of her illness, those who had loved and cared for Mayan as if she were their own mother, yet if considered in the conventional sense they were neither their core family nor their relatives. Therefore, it was inevitable that they too were given a token of her memories. Mayan had now forever blended with the infinite leaving behind her mortal remains; yet, her belongings were now extending into so many homes to be preserved as a token of her remembrance, an inspiration, an awareness and a belief.

□

15

Mayan would often sermonize, "Lend your ear to all, but follow only what your heart says is right. Thereby meaning that one should determine for oneself wherein one's rightful interest lies. Do not mindlessly flow along with the masses. All kinds make up this world. There are those that survive by sheer physical strength and muscle effort, some are controlled by indiscriminate flippancy of the mind while there are some that function by virtue of reasoning and intellect. I always follow the inner voice of my soul as that is of the real substance. Do not follow blind-foldedly, rationalize and then motivate your actions."

Mayan is no longer present in her physical form yet a vivid and real life image of her presence still lives on amongst those who truly loved her.

Bayaji still relives and often narrates so many of those anecdotes that took place during Mayan's lifetime. She narrates them as if they had happened just yesterday.

One such tale was about how a 'sweet pudding' had played a vital role in the fixing of Mayan's marriage. Mayan was always known for her culinary abilities. It so happened that her future father-in-law was so taken up by the mouth watering sweet dish *Halwa* that Mayan had cooked and served him that he had immediately given his consent for her marriage with his son. After the wedding party returned, the new bride and bridegroom were sent off separately accompanied by the groom's young nieces to take a local train to return to their hometown. Mayan was shedding copious tears in memory of her parents and family that she had had to leave behind. Watching her cry, both the young nieces sitting beside her also started crying. Watching them all breakdown like this the poor bridegroom who was the only male person in that group panicked. At a complete loss of what was expected of him, he moved away embarrassed and stood a little apart distancing himself from the emotional drama being played out.

The train slowly grinded to a halt. All the passersby on the railway platform curiously stopped for a second to enquire why the three ladies were crying. The trio was obviously attracting a lot of unnecessary and unwarranted attention. Then someone amongst them noticed the forlorn figure of the groom standing in the corner. As is typical of public behaviour, everyone sympathized with the girls and pointedly reprimanded the bewildered groom for his insensitivity in not taking due care of the ladies. As the train moved on, the trio gradually calmed down as their conversation took off on a different track. One of the nieces commented," Kaki, (aunt) isn't travelling on the train fun?" It was then that they discovered that actually this was Kaki's first train journey. The duo was obviously both intrigued and amused. So taking a mild dig at her ignorance they suggested, "Kaki you better hold on tight to something, else you may be thrown off the train." But pat came Kaki's reply, "Why else do you think I am holding onto you. If we should fall, we'll go down together, won't we?" The atmosphere all around had suddenly lightened as all four had broken into peels of laughter.

The social taboos, reservations were so unique that they often created a comic sequence. For instance, a married couple could not converse directly with each other when there were others present in the vicinity. Therefore, even though they were sitting close to each other yet the conversation between the new couple had to be mediated via the nieces present. So, the husband would suggest, "Kindly inform your Kaki...." but even before the niece could repeat the directions, Kaki would reply, "please tell him that......" The whole situation presented an amusing scenario for the onlookers.

Mayan was really blessed as her mother-in-law doted on her as her own daughter, showering her with loads of love and care. In fact, she would even go to the extent of taking the blame of Mayan's faulty cooking on her own head so that her daughter-in-law was spared from having to face the brunt of severe reprimands that would have otherwise come her way. Mayan had been the darling of her household. So, she was a novice initially as far as cooking and household work was concerned. She could not really differentiate between the various spices needed for cooking. In all fairness, Mayan was really too young to take up the responsibilities of running a household. Mayan virtually learnt everything related to household work from her mother-in-law, who really was a very gracious and an understanding lady.

To narrate another interesting anecdote, once Mayan had fallen sick and there was nobody at home. Pitaji too had been posted elsewhere during those times. The only other family member present in the house was her elder brother-in-law. Realizing that Mayan was rather unwell and could not be left unattended, he found himself in a bit of a fix as it really went against the social norms and accepted behavioural trends if Mayan were to directly address him. Faced with this dilemma of how she would communicate to him if she needed some help or attendance, he finally decided to sleep just outside her bedroom door and as a solution to this very grave problem he tied a long rope around the big toe of his foot. Then, he handed over the other end of the rope to Mayan requesting her, "Please, if you need anything in the night just tug at the string." So this was how he finally managed to find a solution to successfully implement his responsibility. This is another one of those examples of how people in those days would find a suitable solution to both abide by the code of conduct expected of them and at the same time successfully carry out their duties.

This elder brother-in-law in question happened to have three daughters. The mother-in-law had all along nurtured a deep-rooted wish that a boy be born into their family. After Mayan's arrival all her hopes were now pitted on her. She took several measures and extra care to ensure that Mayan was given to eat the so-called recommended diet that would ensure that she would deliver a baby boy. A multitude of herbal concoctions were given to Mayan to savour. But then, God had other plans. Before Mayan could conceive, her elder sister-in-law (the elder brother-in-law's wife) gave birth to a healthy bonny boy as her fourth child. The entire family celebrated and her mother-in-law's joy and excitement really knew no bounds. Bayaji taking advantage of the situation mirthfully jested, "Thank God my mother has delivered a son. Heaven help had she not! God only knows what more concoctions you would have forced upon 'Kaki' then?" She playfully ribbed her grand-mother.

From the very beginning, Mayan and her sister-in-law hit it off really well and had gradually grown close to each other over the years. Not only did they share each other's burdens, but shared their meals and always waited for the other to join in before they would sit to eat. In all the family celebrations Mayan would always take the lead regaling every one with her jests, humour and her amazing dancing and singing prowess. In every wedding in the house, she would take the lead by stepping on to the dance floor and then persuade all the others to join in too. This trait and quality too was another of those innumerable qualities that she had inherited from her mother. Bayaji's face even today lights up when she recollects those moments that Mayan had shared with the family. What a genuine relationship they had shared! In fact, even today the family looks up to their friendship with the due awe and respect it deserves.

Another one of Mayan's unique quality was of being able to prevail upon others even when faced with stiff resistance and in very adverse situations. Pitaji had always had a liking for dishes that had been cooked with garlic and onion added to them for flavour. However, Mayan's mother-in-law looked upon his preference with intense disapproval. Ensuring that the mother-in-law's sentiments were not hurt and at the same time tending to her husband's preference Mayan would often slyly arrange for some garlic and onion gravy dishes to be specially cooked only for him in the courtyard. In fact, Mayan had very often narrated to her sons one of those particular occasion when her mother-in-law had accidentally discovered these under cover going-ons and then how all hell had broken lose. She had used the choicest of expletives to denounce her own son and in the heat of that moment thrown out all those utensils on to the road that had been used for cooking those dishes. It had indeed been one of the most embarrassing moments as the whole neighbourhood had been a witness to this incident.

And that had not been the end of the matter. She had packed her bags ready to leave the son's house threatening never to return. If it had not been for Mayan's intervention the situation would have worsened. Despite the repeated reprimands, her refusal to let go of her bag, all the while begging her not to leave had finally convinced her mother-in-law to stay on. Then running to Pitaji, Mayan had whispered something in his ear. Pitaji, though not in a very compromising mood himself due to his mother's extreme reaction had finally succumbed to Mayan's coaxing and had come forward to ask for his mother's forgiveness, giving the solemn promise that henceforth he would abstain from all such indulgences. It was only then that the mother-in-law had finally calmed down and relented. Yet, never did anyone ever hear Mayan utter a single disrespectful term for either her husband or his mother till she breathed her last.

In fact, the more one were to profess her qualities the more one would not succeed in doing justice to them. She was no doubt the real cementing factor in the family.

As long as her physical strength allowed her she was never found wanting in extending a helping hand to not just her family but to all and sundry. In fact, even after life had taken a serious toll on her physical fitness, making her physically constrained she had still continued to strive on her past life's encumbering issues through sheer mental grit and internal energy and positivity towards life. Then when even that had begun to fail, it was her infallible belief in her God that helped pull her through life's daunting moments. She knew and held the firm belief that man alone could not achieve anything in life if the force of one's conviction in one's 'Faith' ceased to exist. It was this Faith that she held on to till her very last. This is what drove her to deliver unto others with genuine compassion and deep care. No one was ever turned away from her home without a soothing and a comforting gesture, without being offered something to eat, something to drink. For Mayan, a visitor to her house was a representative of God Himself. Therefore, he had to be given the due regard. If ever anything special was cooked in her kitchen, it remained an unbroken custom in her household that part of it was always shared with her relatives and neighbours. She was one of the few in this world who realized the true virtue of sharing and giving. She knew that unless you give and sacrifice, you will forever remain chained to these worldly issues and will never achieve salvation, the final release.

This reminds of an interesting episode that had happened in Mayan's life.

Mayan's family originally hailed from the city of Ajmer in Rajasthan. They had lived there in a rented house for a few years. Rajasthan, largely constituted of desert areas, had always faced scarcity of water. The municipality supplied water for a very limited duration every day. Then to top this even the water pressure in the taps was always pathetic, a slim trickle which barely managed to fill a bucketful of water. The house that they had rented had other tenants occupying it too, so they all had to queue in line to avail of the water supply. Vineet clearly reminiscences that one particular day when due to the delay and lateness in the availability of water Pitaji could not get his meal on time. Consequently, he was delayed in reaching his workplace. This water crisis resulted in an intense argument between Pitaji and the landlord so much so that they came close to exchanging fist cuffs - resulting in a complete severing of communication between them. Now Mayan could not absorb this - after all these were the very people they had shared each day eating, sitting and chatting together for long innumerable hours. The very thought that this healthy harmonious relationship was now about to turn a sour leaf was unbearable to her. Therefore, she lost no time in immediately going over to the landlord's house and humbly imploring, "Dear brother, please have the goodness to overlook this unpleasant exchange. I shall be waiting for you. So, kindly come and join us over a cup of tea." Then turning to his wife she pleaded, "Dear sister, kindly honour my request and join us for tea." Then she quickly retraced her steps and went up to Pitaji, "Please overlook his mistake, forgive him for his failing. Please calm down and for my sake call on him and make him comfortably seated in the drawing room, while I get tea for all of us." That evening did not see just tea being served but an elaborate course of savvy delicacies and sweets as well. Mayan repeatedly piled up their plates with goodies all the while good humouredly insisting that both of them must do justice to the servings. Friendship was once again restored between the two neighbours. In fact, this was not an isolated instance but several more such incidents took place when Mayan was privy to any bitter incident or wherever she felt that even if unwittingly somebody's feelings were hurt, she would immediately empathize with the concerned person and reach out with open arms engulfing them in her tide of compassion and concern. The tension in the environment would then immediately be released. Goodwill and peace would once again prevail.

Though Mayan had never received any formal education, yet there was no dearth of good sense in her along with a very sharp and analytical brain. She was quick witted, full of the zest for life along with a firm determination. She had raised her children in a mould that had turned them into worthy, exemplary human beings with the right values, fortitude and the ability to excel in whatever they took up in life. She held the firm conviction that paying attention to the finest of details was the only way to bring about the right discipline in all the walks of one's life. She thereby provided her children with the right dimensions to develop the ability to think clearly and to bloom. She taught them how to lead a full life, to evolve, to find satisfaction even in paucity, to derive bliss and comfort from even the small benefits of life successfully. She taught them never to forget that it was the Lord above who was the eventual 'Giver'. She drilled in them that they were never to let go of their belief in 'Him' and that 'He' alone was the final decision maker of their destiny. All these values thus had honed them into becoming individuals who could stand up against all the odds that they would have to face in the course of their life.

She had inculcated in her children the ability to remain firm in their belief and to strive on to realize their belief and goal unceasingly.

During the course of the exams of her children, she would forget everything else and devote all her time and energy to ensure that their needs and comforts were attended to primarily. When Vineet had refused to appear for the Civil Services Examination she had been very hurt and upset, "Is it too much to expect from you to fulfil your parents' desire to see you touching great heights in life? My parents did not educate me enough. If they had provided me with the correct exposure to the English language and to education, I would have then accomplished the impossible. Here you are fortunate that your parents are providing you with the right podium to avail this opportunity and you are not realizing it." Sensitive to her pent up frustration and the relevance of the point she was trying to make, Vineet conceded and got down to preparing for the exams. She had then become an incredible force behind him, instilling in him the confidence, goading him, cajoling him on, ensuring that he was provided with proper nutritious food after every little interval and would sometimes press his aching head and his back. She had stood by his side firm and resolute throughout that period. It was evident that she now believed that she would realize the dream that she had nurtured all along through her son. And how she had succeeded!

Mayan not only had a sharp brain but also the keenness of perception to pick things up quickly. Hearing others speak the language, she had picked up quite a few key terms in English to be able to communicate. Beginning with a 'yes', a 'no', a 'please' and a 'thank you', one fine day she managed to surprise all, tickling their bones to the very core. Every one around her had broken out into peels of laughter. It so happened that on one occasion Pitaji had roughed up his grand children severely reprimanding them for misbehaving. But surprisingly, she had immediately come to their defence like a wounded tigress safeguarding her young pups and belligerently chastened Pitaji, "Watch Out, you are really being unfair now. Do not 'overload'. Do not ever in the future say anything to my children. It is so rare to have our house resounding with their merriment and cheer. I do not want you to compel them to become as 'dull and serious' as you yourself have been." Amused by the terminology that she had used, 'overload', her grandkids and her children both kept ribbing her over this unique usage of the word 'overload'. They would say, "grandma, don't you overload me now," then, "grandma you are really overloading me now, better start putting down the load," and they would scamper off giggling. Mayan's reactions were typical of her. She would laugh along pinching their cheeks affectionately, "Ha"! So you will make fun of me. Just you wait I'm coming after you." This was our Mayan at her best, spontaneous and fun loving self. However, on a serious note, is it not a fact that all niggling and overbearing issues in life are a result of 'an overload' – be they associated with physical issues or human emotions like one's uncontrolled ego, cluttering of one's mental thinking and chaotic thought processing.

The values that she had maintained through the entire course of her life were forthrightness, humility, amiability and gentility. That was not to say that she was not capable of a calculated and studied reaction but that surfaced in her only when she was forced to stand up against an opposition that was devious and dishonest. Maybe then to kill a larger vice she may have had to perforce resort to a lesser evil.

A very interesting interlude that had once taken place portrays the strength of her convictions. One day Pitaji had severely rebuked her. She had gone and used Vineet's (who was now a grown up young man) shoulder to cry on, giving vent to her pent up frustration. Naturally reacting to her emotional outburst Vineet had promptly gone to Pitaji's room and taken up her case rather vehemently, expressing his serious disapproval at Pitaji's questionable manner of behaving with his wife. Now, when Mayan heard her son being judgmental about her husband's behaviour, she became furious and losing her cool slapped her grown up son right across his cheek screaming, "How dare you take liberties with your father? Is this what I have taught you, to show disrespect to your elders? Don't you dare speak to your father thus! This is an issue that is between me and your father and we shall resolve it between ourselves."

Still choking with anger Vineet reacted, "But should Pitaji not check his behaviour? Is this the way he should be snubbing you?"

"He will do what he wants. This issue is between us. What gave you the right to question his conduct? You will immediately apologize to him," Mayan had severely chided him further.

His feathers now ruffled, Vineet retreated to his room mumbling under his breath, "This is the limit of injustice. First, she will come crying to me, complaining, and then when I try to extend my support this is what I get in return. Never, never again will I stand up for her. Here I am stretching my neck out for her and I am the one who is being blamed."

Though Vineet, with young blood coursing through his veins, could not realize the magnitude of the strength of her commitment and character - but actually her reaction typically reflected her absolute dedication towards those she loved.

Mayan's actions as well as her thinking repeatedly emphasized her belief that our world lies within us but we often remain oblivious to this fact. One needs to cover this inward journey all by oneself, find one's own path to reach the final destination and all the while carry the burden of one's action and reaction.

Her firm conviction was that God alone decides our destiny. What has to be, will be? So, we should let it prevail and gracefully accept 'His' decision as 'He' has so willed it. That was how she humbly accepted whatever came her way. Today Vineet often reminisces how, while cleaning out the grain, she would often break out into a song in her sweet melodious voice. One of her favorites was:

He who truly immerses himself,
realizing the actual worth of-
the four letter word – 'LOVE';
can then boast of having attained,
the stature of the 'wise and the learned'!!
(Original verses at page 183)

She had a favourite sitting place located just outside the gate of her house where she loved to go and sit in the evening. She would greet any passersby with a warm welcoming smile that would bring a smile on the other's face too making them forget their woes for that moment. What could be a greater gift from one human being to another than to make one forget one's pain, sufferings, handicaps, miseries and share a moment of newly found joy and cheer that would help one to re-energize to face the adversity in their life. The children of the neighbourhood loved to crowd around Mayan in her backyard, all vying to help her to clean the grain, as it meant an afternoon feasting session where the children were offered carrots, guavas, sweetcorn and roasted gram along with jaggery or whatever else that could be made available. The children loved these sessions and while they enjoyed sharing the eats together, Mayan would, without their realizing, it impart invaluable lessons about life to them. She was helping them inculcate the right values in life. This came from a lady who was uneducated but probably had learnt the lessons of life and understood them far better than the so called 'learned'. Her regular preaching to them was, "Learn to live in the present and for the present and not in the future." "What has to be done, do it now, leave nothing for tomorrow for who knows whether we will be there tomorrow." "Do not procrastinate, be positive", "You shall reap what you shall sow," were some of her regular dictums. Whenever she would face a dilemma, she would immediately look for its solution via the saintly scriptures written by the 'Guru' whose disciple she was. She would randomly open a page and whatever it read would be analyzed by her and then connected to the problem on hand. She would then reach a solution and implement it accordingly. Her motto was that it was one's belief that made one discover the ultimate solution to one's problems in life.

Vineet had so often shown his resentment towards this method of coming to a decision. "You really don't realize the gravity of the situation on hand, do you? How can you come to a decision in such an irresponsible way without sensibly reflecting on it, Mayan?"

Then Mayan would respond saying, "Look you first need to consider the pros and the cons. Yet, when all rationale fails you, then draw the inspiration from within you. If your inner self says that it is correct then reflect no more and go ahead with the decision. You shall then see all will be well. Do not unnecessarily worry and contradict yourself." She would then leave it to the person concerned to take the final step.

Another very frequent refrain that came from her was, "Lend your ear to all that is said but hear and act only according to what your heart has to say. Let it be yours and only your decision to decide wherein your true interest lies. Do not follow others blindly. Some follow life's course through sheer physical bull force, some are controlled by the moods of the heart and its flippancy while there are others that use their rationale, their intellect before coming to a decision. As for me, I listen to my inner voice, because to me that is the real essence."

Very often, while talking about Mayan, Anjali would fondly remember her, "Vineet, what a cheerful disposition she had, didn't she? She had the unique ability to rise above any adversity and take the situation head on. To face pain and sufferings with fortitude, persist till she could discover the light at the end of the dark tunnel of adversity was her uniqueness, don't you agree?" Vineet would nod in complete agreement.

These qualities, these abilities stemmed in her via her belief that all adverse situations eventually bring along with them the opportunities for us to learn and grow beyond ourselves. If on some rare occasion her self-confidence did shake, she would convince herself and those around her saying, "God has said that I am there to take over your worries, so why should we worry? Let us carry on with our lives and deliver our duties unafraid. Then what is there for me to worry about? He will help me face what comes my way. Therefore, I put my implicit trust in my Lord and His decisions."

Some of her words would remain unique only to her and sound good coming from her alone. "Point not at others' failings, look unto yours alone. What will be your gain if you should dishearten the other? Learn to stay happy and help others remain happy too, dear." Probably her constant contact with the 'Sants' had given her this wisdom. The crux of her beliefs was as follows – 'Keep a constant check on your behaviour, provide and spread happiness amongst those around and if you should be unable to impart happiness to others, at least do not be a source of their misery either.' She, as long as she lived, remained the cementing force in the family. Her own son-in-law had spontaneously expressed a similar sentiment immediately after she had passed away, "She was the ultimate 'binding force'. God knows what will happen now!" What better and more genuine a praise could come for anyone, anywhere?

In fact, when Vineet had proceeded to start the construction of a small farmhouse a little away from the city, Mayan had been extremely excited about the project and visualised living there. It had been her 'dream house'. So what better tribute could a son pay to his mother, but to name the farmhouse after her! On the eve of her first death anniversary, Vineet had become highly sentimental as all those tender moments that he had shared with her had spilled over in an emotional expression that had come to him spontaneously. And this is his final tribute to her:

You are now an unknown face!
That you happened to be my mother
is the only identity left with me.
The painful consciousness of your departure,
still traverses through the world within me.
You are beyond any recognition now!
Yet the very thought of you-
pierces through my inner self like does the lightening
that strikes the dark.
And then, once again your voice resounds,
enveloping me.
I can still feel you deep within me-
more often during the night-
when I find it so hard to sleep,
due to my aching hands and legs,
which you often stroked so motheringly.
In those culminating days,
you often kept gazing my way,
today I realize you wanted to live some more.
However, you never said a thing,
you never resisted nor complained,

but kept the family bound together like the string
that ties diverse bundle of sticks together.
Today when you are not there,
I often hear those words of yours-
'You shall miss me when I am gone,
as there will be no one to nag and say-
When are you coming back!'
The final truth is that-
you are still vibrant within me,
in your divine form.
I too intend to merge with what
you have surrendered your ultimate self to.
To that which is
infinite, formless and nameless,
'O' my mother!

□

GLOSSARY OF TECHNICAL WORDS

(In alphabetical order)

1. **Acai beri:** An antioxidant, food product found very useful in cancer therapy for elimination / neutralisation of free radicals.
2. **Antacid:** A medicine which neutralises effects of acids in stomach.
3. **Antioxidants:** They neutralise oxidative (free radicals) substance that are harmful for body.
4. **Asparagus:** This plant is helpful in strengthening of immunity, improving digestive system and cleaning body from waste material. Also helps in neutralising cancerous tendencies.
5. **Biopsy:** An operative method to ascertain if nodes are cancerous or not - (operative removal of tumour nodes to confirm cancer).
6. **Blueberry:** A fruit useful in cancer treatment.
7. **Bone density test:** It reveals the amount of calcium in bones. It is used for detection of osteoporosis (weaking of bone).
8. **Chemo port:** A device inserted underneath the skin by minor surgery to deliver chemotherapy doses. This facilitates direct administering of chemo in place of I.V. interventions.

9. **Enzyme:** Fluid secretion from body cells which helps in digestion.
10. **Esiac Tea:** A mixture of four herbs that helps in cancer treatment.
11. **Estrogen receptors:** They are found on the surface of cancer cells. If they are positive, then hormone therapy can be suggested.
12. **Estrogens:** A kind of hormone which helps in progress and spread of Breast cancer.
13. **FISH test:** Florescence in SITU hybridization is a specialised test which maps cancer cells to ascertain nature of cancer.
14. **FNAC:** A technique by which a fine needle is used to take out fluid from tumour to ascertain malignancy by microscopic examination.
15. **Heart Ijection Ratio/Fraction:** Cardiac investigation which shows pumping strength of heart. If ratio is more than 50%, then cancer treatment is given.
16. **Her-2-neu:** Receptor found on surface of cancer cells which characterises virulence of cancer. If found positive than herceptin antibody (immunotherapy) is useful.
17. **Hormone therapy:** Hormonal treatment of cancer.
18. **IHC:** Immuno Hysto chemistry, a special kind of staining technique which reveals type/nature of cancer and ascertains presence of ER, PR and herceptin (a kind of DNA protein).
19. **Imaging:** Radiological examination of internal body parts to know the type of illness by analysis of images e.g. USG, X-RAY, CT SCAN, MRI etc.
20. **Immune system:** A special system of body responsible for enhancing body resistance and protecting the organism from disease. It functions through lymphocytes as well as anti-bodies.

21. **Lymph nodes:** Small, round glands that filters lymph. Cancer augments the lymph nodes.
22. **Lymph system:** Circulates lymph in body. Cancerous cells reach lymph gland through this.
23. **Mammography:** X-Ray of hamalien gland (Breast) for scanning of Breast cancer.
24. **P.R. (progesterone receptor):** Found on the surface of cancerous cell and helps in cancer treatment of P.R. positive patients.
25. **PET:** Positron emission tomography is an imaging device investigation which reveals the growth of cancer in different body parts.
26. **Progesterone:** A hormone that helps in development and spread of breast cancer.
27. **Radiation therapy:** Radio therapy is highly targeted and effective way to destroy cancer cells by radiation.
28. **Receptor:** Found on cell surface and signals growth of cancer cells.
29. **Targeted therapy:** New technique for cancer treatment in which molecular cause of cancer is treated. It is less harmful.
30. **Toxics:** Harmful substance (waste products).

(The above glossary is meant to convey general meaning of the terms as relevant for a common man and does not purport to convey deep technical elaborations on the subject.)

□

GLOSSARY OF HINDI WORDS

(In alphabetical order)

1. **Ahilya:** In Hindu mythology, she was wife of Gautam Maharishi. Cursed and turned into stone, she was liberated by Lord Rama (an incarnation of God Vishnu).
2. **Ayurveda:** A system of traditional medicine native to Indian subcontinent based on codes evolved by 'Charak'; an alternate medicinal system.
3. **Ayurvigyan:** Medical Science.
4. **Bayaji:** In local dialect of Rajasthan, Bayaji means daughter.
5. **Bhaiya:** Brother.
6. **Bhajanghar:** A place or house for meditation.
7. **Bhandara:** A community meal or religious feast held by all the devotees sharing 'Prasad' after a 'bhog' ceremony, experiencing showers of divine grace and mercy through serving each other.
8. **Bhishma Pitamah:** Blessed with wish-long life, the main character of Mahabharata struggled to bring unity between Pandvas and Kaurvas, his grand nephews.
9. **Bhog:** Culminating submissions or offerings before the deity or the divine; also relevant in context of Prasad (see Prasad).
10. **Brahma:** Hindu God of creation.
11. **Dharmaraj Yudhishthir:** In the Hindu epic Mahabharata, he is known as the righteous king or king

of 'Dharma'. Yudhishthir means 'steady in war'.

12. **Guru:** The spiritual messenger of the Divine who has elevated to the higher spiritual regions and, therefore, empowered to guide the devotees in the spiritual journey; a spiritual parent or teacher.
13. **Gurudwara:** Gateway to Guru, place where Guru resides or holds his 'Satsang'.
14. **Hazaratji:** In the book it has been used in context of Hazarat Abraham known for performing sacrifice (Qurbani) of his son following God's command.
15. **Himalaya:** Mountain range in Indian subcontinent which is home to the planet's highest peaks.
16. **Kabir:** Propounder of the Sant Mat, regarded as the initial Supreme Saint and widely acclaimed for his tenets across different sects (also see Sant Mat).
17. **Kaki:** In local dialect in Rajasthan, Kaki is 'Chachi', the wife of father's younger brother.
18. **Karmas:** Indian religious concept of action or deeds woven throughout the entire cycle of cause and effect of a soul's reincarnated lives.
19. **Khuda:** 'God' or 'Lord'.
20. **Krishna:** As per Hindu belief he was the full incarnation of Supreme God Vishnu (God who sustains, preserves and governs the universe).
21. **Lala:** A lovable son.
22. **Lalli:** A lovable daughter.
23. **Ma:** Mother.
24. **Mahabharata:** One of the two major Sanskrit epics of ancient India, the other being Ramayana.
25. **Mahajan:** People involved in business of money lending.
26. **Mahamritunjaya Jap:** Holy rendition of verses, as per Hindu belief, to prevent untimely death; a death conquering mantra (a set of holy syllables).
27. **Maharaj:** Guru; spiritually superior person.

28. **Malik:** Used to address God, the controller, owner.
29. **Mataji:** Respectfully addressing a Mother.
30. **Mayan:** A generic term for 'mother' in Rajasthan.
31. **Meera Bai:** One of the Hindu saints known for her devotion towards Lord Krishna and her devotional poetry [mystic poet, Vaishnav Bhakti Movement]
32. **Nani:** Maternal grandmother.
33. **Pallu:** An edge of a garment.
34. **Pitaji:** Respectfully addressing a Father.
35. **Prasad:** A material substance, usually an edible food, which is first offered to the deity and then distributed to the devotees or followers as a good sign, considered to have deity's blessings residing within it; 'divinely-invested'.
36. **Radha:** See Radhasoami.
37. **Radhasoami:** The Holy name 'Radhasoami' represents the 'Supreme Being' as propounded by the founder of the Faith. This faith is founded on the principles of Sant Mat (see Sant Mat). The original seat of the faith is at Soamibagh, Agra. Intrinsically the word depicts the divine confluence of 'Radha', the soul in the purest original form or in its prime current and the 'Soami', the formless, spaceless and nameless conglomeration of the absolute and infinite consciousness.
38. **Rajasthan:** A state of India in the north-west part of the country, known for sagas of bravery, rich culture, architectural heritage and natural desert beauty.
39. **Sant Mat:** Spiritual movement, the nature of knowledge, emanating from those saints who have elevated to the highest spiritual region and thus are in a position to guide us through the spiritual journey; the basic tenets revolve around renunciation of worldly attachments and holding on to the spiritual current, depicted through divine light and sound, and meditate along to elevate one's soul. The religion of Saints

propounding *Surat* (self-absorbed intelligent energy; spirit) – *Shabad* (current of the real essence) *Yoga*. (This philosophy is of Indian origin and repeatedly propounded by galaxy of spiritually elevated Saints)

40. **Sari:** A garment of woman in India.
41. **Satsang:** Association with the highest 'Truth' through a 'guru' (the messenger of the divine) or assembly of devotees who listen to and assimilate the 'truth' through scriptures, meditate and bring their meaning to life. Inward Satsang is the company of the spiritual current within, which consists of listening to spiritual sounds or in articulating internally the spiritual names or an earnest and affectionate contemplation of the form of the spiritual Guru or remembrance of His gracious acts.
42. **Shabad:** A piece of holy text in Indian Culture; the divine sound; the regenerative spiritual current.
43. **Shiva:** Shiva is the Hindu deity and considered to be the Supreme God and also known as 'destroyer' or 'transformer'.
44. **Soami:** Supreme Being. Aslo see Radhasoami.
45. **Tandava:** Divine dance performed by Hindu God 'Shiva' that is the source of cycle of creation, preservation and dissolution.
46. **Vaidyaraj:** A practitioner of Ayurvedic medicines.

□

HOLY VERSES

(As quoted in the book)

Page 108-09

Darsan deeje naam sanehi,
tum bin dukh pave meri dehi.
Dukhit tum bin, ratat nis din,
pargat darsan deejiye.
Binti sun priya swamiya,
bali jaaun, vilamb naa keejiye

—Kabir

Page 113

Haman hai ishk mastana,
haman ko hoshiyaari kya.
Rahein aazad ya jag mein,
haman duniya se yaari kya.
Jo bichude hain piyare se,
bhatekte dar badar phirte.
Hammara yaar hai hum mein,
haman ko intezaari kya.
Na pal bichude piya humse,
na hum bichude piyaare se,
Unhi se neh laagi hai,
haman ko bekarari kya.
Kabira ishk ka maata,

dui ko door kar dil se.
Jo chalna rah nazuk hai,
haman sar bojh bhaari kya.

—Kabir

Page 125

Avinashi dulha kab milihon,
bhaktan ke rakhpal.
Hum to tumhari daasi sajna,
tum humre bhartaar.
Deendayal daya kar aao,
samrath surjan haar.
Kai hum praan tajtu hain pyaare,
kai apni kari lev,
Das Kabir birah ati baadhyo,
ab to darshan dev.

—Kabir

Page 132

Aankh, kaan, muhun band karao,
anhad jhinga shabd sunao.

Page 133-34

Sukirat kar le naam sumiri le, ko jaane kal ki,
jagat mein khabar nahi pal ki.
Jhoot kapat kari maya jorin, baat karen chall ki,
paap ki poat dhare sir upar, kis vidhi hai halki.
Yeah man toh hai hasti masti, kaya mitti ki,
saans saans mein naam sumiri le, awadhi ghate tan ki.
Kaya andar hansa bole, khushiyan kar dil ki,
jab yeh hansa nikari jaahinye, maati jungle ki.
Kaam, krodh madd lobh bisaro, yaahi baat asal ki,
Gyan bairag, daya man raakho, kahe kariba dil ki.

Page 134, 146

Ghar ko chod adhar ko chaali,
surat hansini aaj bhai.

—Radhasoami Santmat

Page 134

Tumhari chinta main mann dhaari,
tum achint reh dharo piyaara.

—Radhasoami Santmat

Page 154

Tum palak ughado Dinanath,
haazir- naazir kab ki khadi.
Sau the dusman hoi laage
sab ne langu kadi,
Tum bin sau kou nahi hai,
digi nav meri samund adi.
Din nahi chain raat nahin nidra,
sukhun khadi khadi.
Baan birah ke lage hiye mein,
bhoolun na ek ghadi.
Pathhar ki toh Ahilya taari,
ban ke beech padi.
Kaha bojh Meera mein kahiye,
sou uppar ek dhadri.

Page 169

Dhai aakhar prem ka,
pade so pandit hoye.

—Kabir

□□□